"Tiffany," he said,
"I need a wife."

Ben didn't give her time to answer before he continued. "My father's health would improve if he could stop worrying about my single state. Your aunt could get off her hobbyhorse about finding you a suitable husband...."

Tiffany was reluctant, but she saw no way out of her predicament. The staff at Coronet Airlines all thought that their fellow workers, Ben a̶ ̶f̶any, were planning to marry, e̶ ̶ ̶ e knew the truth behind th̶ ̶ ̶ ̶ ̶ ere was Aunt Marge̶ ̶

"I need time to ̶ ̶ ̶ ̶ said.

"I'll give you ̶ ̶ ̶ k this evening," ̶ ̶ gh it were all so simpl̶ ̶ nd made up one way ̶ ̶ hen...." And off he went.

OTHER
Harlequin Romances
by JESSICA STEELE

Many of these titles are available at your local bookseller.

For a free catalogue listing all available Harlequin Romances,
send your name and address to:

HARLEQUIN READER SERVICE,
M.P.O. Box 707, Niagara Falls, N.Y. 14302
Canadian address: Stratford, Ontario, Canada N5A 6W2

Turbulent Covenant

by

JESSICA STEELE

Harlequin Books

TORONTO • LONDON • LOS ANGELES • AMSTERDAM
SYDNEY • HAMBURG • PARIS • STOCKHOLM • ATHENS • TOKYO

Original hardcover edition published in 1980
by Mills & Boon Limited

ISBN 0-373-02355-3

Harlequin edition published September 1980

Printed in U.S.A.

CHAPTER ONE

It had been a good flight. The mammoth aircraft had brought them to fine weather in London. A little cold perhaps, especially after the brilliant sunshine of Australia, but a welcome change from the November drizzle they had left in London less than a week before.

To Tiffany Nicholls, stewardess with Coronet Airlines, November might just as well have lived up to its reputation and been dull and foggy. Try as she might she just could not lift the feeling of despondency which had been with her since the day they had taken off Australia-bound.

Mechanically she had carried out her duties, had been pleasant and helpful to the passengers on board, her natural sensitivity masking the ache within her. She'd tried hard to put Nick Cowley out of her thoughts, but no matter how hard she tried his face would appear again and again—How could she have been so wrong about him?

Again she saw his good-looking face and her eyes took on a wounded, haunted look as she thought, not for the first time, how certain she had been that he was sincere. Theirs was not a fleeting attraction, she had thought their relationship had been deep and meaningful. Nick hadn't exactly asked her to marry him, but it had been understood between them—so she thought.

Tiffany bit fretfully at her bottom lip, and was so deep in her memories that it came as something of a shock to find the captain of the aircraft at her elbow, and to find her memories being rudely interrupted by his brusque:

'Would you mind stepping out of the way—I'd like to get by.'

Tiffany came to, to realise she was still standing in the doorway after seeing the last passenger off. There was room for Captain Maxwell to squeeze by, as big as he was, but the look on his face as his eyes flicked over her curves told her, while other men might find her attractive, if he had his way he wouldn't come within ten yards of her. Hastily she moved to one side, a slight pink coming up under her skin. She had never liked the man, but he needn't make it so obvious he couldn't bear the sight of her either.

Ben Maxwell moved as though to step through the opening and then down the stairway, but paused and looked down at her as she blanked all expression from her face.

'A word of advice, Nicholls.' The use of her surname told her whatever advice he had for her was not going to be anything she wanted to hear, though she could never remember him calling her by her first name anyway, but she looked steadily back into his cold grey eyes, the training she had making her hold her tongue when what she would like to have done was to tell him what he could do with any advice he had for her, but when he continued with, 'Learn to handle your love life,' the faint pink in her cheeks turned to scarlet as he hit at the very heart of her.

'How did ...?' came spurting from her before she realised he couldn't possibly know her love life had collapsed around her, and that his suggestion was purely the result of extremely good guesswork.

'How did I know?' he finished for her. 'I'd have to be blind not to—— Snap out of it, Nicholls,' he told her harshly. 'If you can't handle your love life, at least have the good manners not to bore the rest of us with your dramatics.'

All Tiffany's training went for nothing as she opened her mouth to retaliate in furious anger, but before one solitary word could leave her, Ben Maxwell was already descending the steps and striding across the tarmac.

It was beneath her to yell after him, she decided, as she glared at his departing back. Oh, how she hated him! Who did he think he was? Being one of the best pilots Coronet had didn't give him the right to be so downright rude. She joined the other stewardesses and went about her duties, her whole body seething. I just hope your love life turns sour on you one day, Captain Benedict Maxwell! she fumed silently, and felt helpless with the frustration of knowing it never would. Not only was he capable and in command of any aircraft he flew, she was sure he was more than able to handle any emotional crisis that came into his life—though knowing him, he was too hard, too cold, to let emotions play any part in his life.

Dramatics indeed! She could have understood his stinging comments if she'd flung her arms about, gone into a swoon, or collapsed into tears every time somebody spoke to her, but she hadn't; she had gone about her work efficiently and quietly as she had been trained to do. I hope you get yours, she thought mutinously, and turned to see her friend and fellow stewardess Patti Marshall had come to join her in the galley.

'Nearly finished?' Patti enquired, looking round to see if there was anything else that needed doing. There wasn't. 'Lord, I'm tired.'

'Have I been any different this trip?' Tiffany asked her after giving a quick look round to see everything was in apple pie order.

'Different?' Patti queried. 'No, I don't think so—you've

been quiet, of course, but then you're not a noisy person, are you? Why do you ask?'

'Oh, nothing.' Tiffany didn't want to reveal any of her conversation with Ben Maxwell to Patti, though she could trust her not to repeat anything she told her. 'Just something Ben Maxwell said, that's all.'

'Oh-oh,' said Patti, her infectious grin coming to the fore. 'If there is anything different about you, you can trust old eagle-eye Maxwell to spot it—I say, you're all right, aren't you? I mean, there's nothing wrong, is there ...?' Patti's face took on a concerned look which didn't sit well on her usually happy smiling face.

'No ...' Tiffany began, then realising she would rather Patti heard it from her than anyone else, for everyone's private life didn't stay private for very long with the tightly knit group of Coronet, 'N-Nick and I have split up.' There, it was out. The secret she had been nursing all week.

'Oh, Tiffany, I'm sorry!' Patti was instantly sympathetic. She knew how head over heels in love with Nick Cowley her friend was, and even though in her opinion he was nowhere near good enough for her, she couldn't help but feel sorry for the pain Tiffany was feeling. Patti looked uncomfortable as a thought suddenly struck her. 'Your break-up with Nick didn't—er—have anything to do with what I said, did it?'

'Of course not,' Tiffany denied quickly.

Then there was no time for further conversation, for the Customs and Excise men were on board making their routine check of the stores and paper work, and Tiffany finally made her way to the staff car park without having another word with Patti.

She had told Patti her split with Nick had nothing to do with anything she had said, but if Patti hadn't said,

'Watch what you get up to, duckie,' when she had told her she was going away for the weekend with Nick, the break with him would not have come as soon as it had. Tiffany faced squarely that she ought to be grateful to Patti, and in a way she was, because Patti's careless remark had saved her from making an even bigger fool of herself, she thought as she drove to her apartment.

Nick had made it sound so romantic when he'd suggested they go away for the weekend. Just the two of them, he had said. Nick's father owned a light engineering business which kept him too busy to make frequent trips to the weekend cottage he owned in Wales. He had asked Nick to go down and give the place an airing, and Nick had waited until Tiffany had been able to get a long weekend off—Bookings had slackened off now that the holiday rush was over, and she had been delighted at the idea of spending three days solely in Nick's company.

She had been looking forward to it so much she just had to tell somebody, and Patti was the obvious person to tell. But Patti's casually voiced, 'Watch what you get up to, duckie,' had planted the first doubts as to the innocence of the weekend.

'Oh, it won't be anything like that,' she had told Patti confidently, fully expecting Patti to agree with her.

Only Patti hadn't agreed with her, and the smile had left her face. 'Oh, Tiffany, you're so hopelessly naïve,' she had sighed despairingly.

'But it won't be like that,' Tiffany remembered arguing stoutly. 'Nick ...'

Patti cut her off short. 'Ask him,' she'd urged. 'Just ask him, Tiffany.'

She hadn't wanted to ask him anything of the sort. Patti might think she was naïve, but she didn't think so herself. Oh, she knew other girls might go away for the weekend with a man and act as though they were man and wife, but she'd been going out with Nick for some time now, and Nick knew she couldn't be like that. He understood that while she might thrill to being in his arms, fully enjoy his kisses, that when their lovemaking threatened to go beyond that stage, something, a kink she must have inherited from somewhere, stopped her from going any further. Nick had been puzzled by it at first, but when he had discovered there wasn't any way round it, he had accepted it—or so she had thought—and called her a sweet old-fashioned thing.

So while knowing the weekend in Wales would be just as innocent as she had originally thought before Patti had planted the seed of doubt in her mind, Tiffany plucked up courage to ask Nick, knowing he would laugh at her, be amused by her anxiety. But her world had fallen apart to find he hadn't been amused. Astounded. Disbelieving. But definitely not amused.

'You're not serious, Tiffy?' he'd asked, as though doubting he was hearing alright. 'Oh, for God's sake—surely you didn't think the weekend was going to be a Sunday school trip?' And noticing she had grown pale, her face troubled, 'It'll be all right, lover—nothing can go wrong. We'll have a fabulous time, honestly we will.'

He had made a grab for her, but she had evaded his arms. She had to think. Think clearly. The worst thing was she still wanted to go—wanted to feel his arms about her. But wasn't he treating the whole thing too lightheartedly? Didn't he *know* she couldn't make that sort of commitment without some very deep soul-searching—didn't he understand the first thing about her? She had thought they were so close, yet here she was doubting his sincerity. He had told her often of his love for her, yet suddenly she had found herself doubting those words of love. And then, with blinding clarity, so sharp she had wanted to hide away from it, she knew Nick Cowley had never loved anybody but Nick Cowley, and that the weekend away with him would not be a weekend of growing to know each other better, a weekend where they could discover things about each other that had remained hidden in the company of other friends. They'd had some good times together, she acknowledged, but she saw at that moment that Nick wouldn't miss her if she went out of his life for ever, while she . . .

'I'm sorry, Nick, I can't come with you.'

It had nearly broken her saying those words, even as she said them she was hoping she was mistaken in her sudden belief that this was the end. No longer would she be able to look forward to seeing him. Never again would she race out of the staff car park on her return from trips all over the globe and rush to meet him.

'Don't be wet, lover,' he had wheedled. 'It's happening all the time—couples are always going away together.' Her face had felt frozen as the implication of what couples went away for hit her—she had thought she and Nick were different. Nick had seen from her face that she couldn't be moved, and the smile had vanished from his face as he had sneered, 'You can't be a virgin all your life.'

His words had taken away any vestige of doubt she had still been nursing. She should have been angry, should have hit out at him, if not with her hands, then at least verbally, but she had done neither. She had just felt dreadfully sick and had run away from him before he had seen just what his words had done to her.

When she was a child family upsets, and there had always been plenty of those, had caused her to be physically sick. Her sensitivity was such that the anguish of her feelings had found an outlet in a stomach reaction. She had thought she had grown out of it. It had stopped happening when her parents had divorced and she had gone to live with her aunt, but on reaching the sanctuary of her flat, whatever had been between her and Nick as good as buried, she knew the malady of her childhood was still with her and she had only just made it to the bathroom in time. She had left the bathroom to go and lie on her bed and force her mind not to relive the scene with Nick.

It had been what she needed to be called out on duty. Ironically, her weekend had been cancelled as several of the other stewardesses had gone down with a virus infection.

It had had to be Captain Benedict Maxwell in charge of the aircraft en route for Australia. Ben Maxwell, Tiffany now fumed. There had to be a fly in everyone's ointment, and he just happened to be hers. From the word go they had never hit it off, but there had been no need for him to be so cuttingly rude to her. Tiffany stayed her thoughts. Patti had said she had been quiet, but she hadn't thought she had been any more quiet than usual, but ... Had her sole preoccupation with thoughts of Nick interfered with her work? She had been sure it hadn't, though ... Tiffany didn't want Ben Maxwell to be right—she cast him out of her mind; she wouldn't give him another thought.

She was glad to reach her flat, park her car and let herself in. Janet on the first floor had her spare key, she'd go down and see her later. Unbuttoning the dark blue jacket of the Airline issue of her suit, Tiffany slipped out of her shoes and stretched tiredly as she made for the bathroom. Soon she had the bath water running and was looking forward to a ten-minute soak. But before she got that far the phone in the sitting room rang. Nick, was her first thought, though she knew it wouldn't be him. It wasn't. Tiffany straightaway recognised her aunt Margery's voice.

'I haven't heard from you, dear,' her aunt reminded her. Tiffany loved her aunt dearly, and about to explain she had just got in, had her reply taken completely from her mind as her aunt went on, 'And how is that young man of yours?'

Oh God, she had forgotten she'd told her aunt everything about having a steady boy-friend. To have done so underlined how sure she had been at the time that Nick's avowal of love meant that he intended to ask her to marry him. She couldn't face just yet telling her the romance was off, and didn't know what she replied in answer to her question into Nick's health as she avoided saying anything that would distress her aunt. But whatever she had answered must have satisfied her, because she went on, her voice warm and full of love for her niece:

'Has he proposed to you yet?'

Her aunt's question thundered into Tiffany's brain, while part of her registered that she had left the bath taps running and if she didn't go and turn them off, Janet below would soon be flooded out. With cold, frightening shock, Tiffany realised she must have answered 'Yes', to her aunt's question of had Nick proposed. Quickly she opened her mouth to retract that statement, but her aunt was even quicker, as a sound of pure delight reached Tiffany's ears over the wires.

'Oh, darling, I'm so happy for you! I doubt there's a happier woman anywhere. When is the wedding to be?'

Tiffany was panic-stricken at the rapture in her aunt's voice, and the words to tell her she was no longer going out with Nick just wouldn't leave her throat. Her aunt had been convinced that her spinster state at the age of twenty-four was the direct result of the effect of the cat and dog life Tiffany's parents had led prior to their divorce eight years ago. And now, Tiffany thought, her aunt was in the seventh heaven to think it had left no permanent mark on her.

'I'm so thrilled, darling,' Margery Bradburn was saying softly again. 'You never did get round to telling me his name—what is it?'

Tiffany's mind registered that her aunt was asking her to tell her the name of the man she had just agreed had asked to marry her. 'I – er – I shall have to go, Aunty, my bath will be running over.' She knew it was cowardly, but she couldn't carry on with this conversation. She would have to put the phone down and sort out how to retract her statement later without causing her aunt too much upset.

'All right, dear. I know you want to go and make yourself beautiful for your young man—— Does he fly too?'

'Y ... Yes.' That was another 'Yes' too many. She wished she could put the phone down, wished she could tell her aunt honestly what happened. Dear Aunt Margery, she thought, why am I such a coward when it comes to hurting you? Why can't I just come out and tell you it's all finished? All she had to say was a short, 'It's all off', but she couldn't. Not with her aunt sounding so overjoyed.

'You didn't tell me his name, dear,' Margery Bradburn reminded her gently.

His name? Tiffany sought round for a name to give her aunt, unwittingly entering further into deceiving her, her main object being to get off the phone in order to compose some story that wouldn't be too painful for her aunt to hear. She needed a name and quick, and could think of none but Nick Cowley—any name but Nick Cowley would do.

'Ben Maxwell,' she said. Then her aunt was telling her cheerfully to run along and have her bath, and she was left holding the receiver, her aunt gone.

Tiffany stared at the telephone with a look of horror on her face. She hadn't said Ben Maxwell, had she? She hadn't, she couldn't have—had she? What had possessed her? Oh, God! She couldn't help a weak smile, he'd just love that. Big, strong, he-man type Ben Maxwell, he would just love to know the girl he thought bad-mannered, dramatic and unable to handle her love life had just claimed him as her fiancé.

Tiffany had three days rest before her next flight. Three days in which to contact her aunt and confess that she no longer had a boy-friend. Three days in which to confess that she barely knew Ben Maxwell, let alone was engaged to him.

More than once her hand went to the telephone, and on one occasion she actually dialled her aunt's number, only to faintheartedly replace the receiver. Half a dozen times she tried to write, but just couldn't get the words to look right on paper.

It was on the last of her rest days that she decided there was nothing for it but she would have to go down to Middledeane and tell her aunt face to face. It was too late now, she wouldn't have time to get there and back, but she would make it her first priority when she returned from her next flight. It was not going to be easy; Tiffany felt her aunt's anguish as her own, and inwardly groaned. Aunt Margery was a dear, but she did have this bee in her bonnet about her and marriage.

She recalled when she had first become aware of it, she had been eighteen at the time and had been living with her aunt for about two years then. She had returned home after being at a dance with Geoff Cooper, a young man only a little older than herself. She had enjoyed her even-

ing, and after saying goodnight to him at the door had
gone into the sitting room to find her aunt still up. That in
itself was unusual enough for her to comment on, for it
was her aunt's habit to be in bed by ten-thirty, and it had
been nearly midnight then.

'Not in bed yet, Aunty?'

'I thought you might be bringing your young man in for
coffee,' had been her aunt's reply.

Tiffany had bubbled into gentle laughter. 'My young
man, Aunty!—I've only been out with him once, and I
doubt if I shall be going out with him again.' This was
because Geoff Cooper was off to university the very next
day.

She had expected her aunt to smile in return, but instead
she had shown how very upset she was at her reply. 'Oh,
Tiffany, I hope you haven't told him you don't want to see
him again.' And before Tiffany could answer, she had
gone on to say that all marriages were not like her parents'
and that Tiffany should not allow the unpleasant memories
of the fiasco her parents' marriage had been to warp her
outlook.

Astonished, because her aunt's fears were unnecessary,
Tiffany stared at her, trying to understand her anxiety.
Aunt Margery's marriage had been a particularly happy one
before her unfortunate widowhood a short time before
she had gone to live with her. Tiffany had tried to quiet
her aunt's fears by telling her that life with her parents
had left her with no prejudicial feelings one way or the
other, but her aunt had remained unconvinced.

Over the next three years a pattern had emerged of her
aunt first impressing on her the good points of her various
escorts, then warming to the theme of what a good husband
this one or that one would make. Tiffany had never argued
with her, though she tried to get her to see that she wasn't

interested in marriage purely for the sake of it, but had failed and only succeeded in further convincing her that she did have a marriage hang-up. So weakly, probably because she was so very fond of her, Tiffany had let the mountain that should have stayed a molehill grow, until now it was out of all proportion. She was reasonably good-looking, having long dark hair, wide brown eyes and a clear creamy skin, and had on occasions been called beautiful by one or two male acquaintances, but in her view she felt she would marry if and when she fell in love, and only then. Pain hit her as she forced thoughts of Nick from crowding into her mind.

At twenty-one she had joined Coronet Airlines, had done her six weeks training, and had been flying ever since, first on short-haul routes and when more experienced she had been put on long-haul routes. It was hard, tiring work, but she loved every minute of it. She got on well with most people she came into contact with. Passengers and crew seemed to like her—Ben Maxwell was the exception, but she had decided not to think about *him* either.

It had been a wrench leaving her aunt and Middledeane, but she had felt it was something she had to do—her regret at leaving Aunt Margery had been tempered with a feeling of adventure, a feeling of standing on her own two feet. The first six months away from Middledeane had been spent sharing a flat with three other stewardesses, but being in some ways a loner, she had looked for a place of her own and the other girls had no difficulty in finding another fourth when Tiffany had moved.

Yes, she loved this flat, Tiffany decided as she placed her uniform cap at its correct angle on top of her French pleat before picking up her case and taking a last look round. She would be on duty shortly and it came to her automatically to check all electricity was off, plugs taken from their sockets and the gas fire off before she left.

Pulling the door behind her, Tiffany descended to the flat below where Janet and Bill Thompson lived. Janet would keep an eye on her flat and Tiffany knew she was happy to hold her spare key in case of burst pipes or the like. Janet would always pop up and put her immersion heater on ready for when she came back. It was an old house and anything could happen, from tiles falling off the roof to window frames working loose.

Only yesterday, she mused, as she waited for Janet to answer her knock, she had been along to the estate agents who handled the property for her landlord, Mr West, to report a broken sash cord.

Janet as usual was ready for a long chat, but seeing Tiffany in the blue and gold of her uniform knew she wouldn't have time for a gossip.

'How long will you be away?'

'It's a three-week trip.' Tiffany tried to infuse some pleasure into the thought of the round the world trip in front of her, but it was hard going. Damn Nick!

Happily Janet was unaware that Tiffany and Nick had split up and chattered happily away until Tiffany found a polite moment to interrupt her.

'I must go, Janet.'

'I'll pop up and switch the immersion on,' Janet offered. 'Three weeks tomorrow?'

It was nice having Janet and Bill below, Tiffany thought as she headed down the next flight of stairs. They got on well and occasionally she was able to repay their kindness in keeping an eye on her flat, by baby-sitting with their three-year-old son Andrew. Tiffany bumped into Miss Tucker, the elderly ground floor tenant, on her way out, and stopped to have a word with her. 'Take care, Miss

Nicholls,' Miss Tucker said as Tiffany hurried through the front door. Tiffany smiled; Miss Tucker didn't trust airplanes, they weren't natural.

The next three weeks went by in a flash. After Ben Maxwell's admonishment of her—thank goodness he wasn't the captain this trip—Tiffany took great care no one should know the mental anguish she was going through. She was even able to answer Dusty Miller, a navigator, when he asked, 'Is that Nick chap still taking up all your free time?' with a 'Who's Nick?' without Dusty being aware that the sound of Nick's name made her flinch inside. It was all Dusty needed, however, and he made a point of being near her when she went sightseeing with some of the others.

By the time they disembarked at the airport in Calcutta, Tiffany had come to terms with herself. Nick was finished. Over. He wouldn't be getting in touch with her again, but just supposing he did, she had firmly made up her mind to refuse to go out with him. She hadn't stopped loving him, even telling herself his declared love for her was without substance, couldn't stop her from loving him. It wasn't that easy. How long would he have continued to date her if she had given in to his desires? Her cheeks flamed at the thought of what she would have committed herself to—how would she ever have been able to look Aunt Margery in the face afterwards? She'd buy her something really nice while she was in India. How could she have deceived her for one minute by letting her believe she was engaged to someone called Ben Maxwell? The sooner that slip of the tongue was rectified the better.

It was quite warm when they touched down in London— warm for December, that was. It had been an exhausting three weeks and Tiffany was glad it had been so. She left the aircraft and shortly afterwards was saying good-

bye to the small band of stewardesses collected by the staff
notice board. She made her way to the car park and was
nearly up to her Mini, her car keys already in her hand,
when glancing down the line of parked cars, she froze in
absolute horror.

She couldn't believe what she was seeing and blinked
twice in rapid succession. Then all colour drained from
her face and she had to put a hand to the nearest car to
steady herself. For there, standing smiling and talking,
was not only her aunt Margery who by rights should be in
Middledeane, but the over-large man she was smiling and
talking with was none other than Captain Benedict
Maxwell.

Oh God, no—— How had she got here? What ... ?
Who ... ? Tiffany's thinking power threatened to cave in
as the thought tumbled in that she would be completely
and utterly humiliated if her aunt had told Ben Maxwell
he was engaged to be married to the stewardess he just
couldn't stand.

Ben Maxwell was just about to hand her aunt into
his car when her aunt looked across and saw her. Tiffany's
feet, after her initial shock, had taken wings, and by that
time she was about only twenty yards away and drawing
nearer, her one thought to get her aunt away from Ben
Maxwell before she could say anything that would make
him heap coals of wrath down on her head and also make
Tiffany Nicholls the laughing stock of Coronet Airlines.

She hated having to hurt her aunt this way, but there
was nothing else for it. Fully determined to *drag* her
away if necessary, Tiffany covered the remaining yards at
a sprint, and opened her mouth to speak, only to close it
again as a firm grip descended on her arms and she felt
herself being mercilessly hauled up against Ben Maxwell's
hard frame. The pressure of his hands on her arms in-

creased as he felt her instinctive pull to get away from
him and she knew without asking that he wasn't going to
let her go until he was good and ready.

She stifled a groan as the thought of how much Aunt
Margery had told him shot through her. He was a good
eight inches taller than Tiffany, and slowly as if in a
trance she let her gaze travel upwards, though terrified of
what she would read in his eyes. Her eyes took in his
iron-hard chin, travelled up to his unsmiling mouth—no
suggestion of humour there, perhaps a hint of sensuality
in his bottom lip—her eyes journeyed up past his straight
nose, and unwillingly came to rest as she looked into steely,
ice cold grey eyes. She wanted to look away, but couldn't.
Wanted to move away, but he held her immobile against
him. She could feel his cool breath on her cheeks as he
returned her look, and would dearly loved to have fainted
at that moment, but she had never fainted in her life. For
the moment she had forgotten her aunt was standing there
with them, and she wondered afterwards how long Ben
Maxwell would have gripped her against him, if her aunt's
voice hadn't penetrated between them.

'It isn't every day one sees a girl racing to greet her
fiancé, is it, Mr Maxwell?' Tiffany heard her aunt say, and
wondered as the words hit her, and with them the knowledge that dragging her aunt away would be useless now,
if with the crimson colour of embarrassment staining her
cheeks any attempt she made to pretend to faint would
be believed.

She bit her lip in mortification as she resisted the
temptation to try it anyway. This was something that would
still have to be faced even after she had come round from
her pretended faint. This situation wasn't going to go
away—there was no way out of it. Here, in front of Ben
Maxwell, she was going to have to confess to her aunt

that he wasn't, never had been, and that pigs would fly before he ever got himself engaged to her. Aunt Margery was going to be hurt and Ben Maxwell would probably make mincemeat of her, but there was nothing else for it.

The pressure on her arms lifted and she found that while he still held on to her with one hand, as though thinking the minute she was free she would make a dash for the nearest bolthole, her other arm was free so that she could turn and face her happy smiling aunt. She lifted her head proudly; whatever Ben Maxwell thought of her, she would get her explanations over with as much dignity as she could muster.

'Aunty . . .' she began, but got no further. Unbelievably, Ben Maxwell was replying to her aunt's comment about his fiancée racing into his arms.

'Well, it is some time since we've seen each other, isn't it, *dear?* And we have such a lot to talk about.' His grip on her arm tightened as he switched his glance to Tiffany. '*Haven't we?*'

Tiffany definitely didn't like the way he said that 'Haven't we?' and she gave another imperceptible pull to get away from him. It was a wasted effort. Ben Maxwell wasn't ready to let her go, and he was calling the tune.

'I have one or two loose ends to clear up,' he told her. Tiffany noticed then that his travel holdall was placed by the door of his car, so he had more than likely landed in London not very long ago himself. 'I'll call for you at the usual time—we'll have a bite of dinner somewhere.' The bruising pressure on her arm increased, forcing her to acquiesce.

'Yes, all r-right,' Tiffany stammered, incapable of coherent thought. She couldn't understand why he hadn't given her away. He wasn't liking this any more than she was, and he certainly didn't like her sufficiently to want to cover up for her. Could it be he had finer feelings than she had given him credit for and that he was doing so from a feeling of not wanting to hurt her aunt?

Tiffany looked at her aunt and saw her eyes were brimming over with tears. Ben Maxwell chose that moment to relax his hold on her arm, and Tiffany wrenched herself away from him and put her arm around Margery Bradburn's shoulders.

'Don't be upset, darling,' she said gently, unable to bear seeing her aunt in tears. Her eyes met Ben Maxwell's over her aunt's shoulders. His expression was inscrutable, and Tiffany hurriedly turned her attention back to the motherly woman who was fighting to keep the tears back.

'I'm so happy for you, Tiffany—I was so sure you'd decided never to marry.'

Tiffany forced a smile as her aunt dried her tears, and her arms fell away from her shoulders. What a mess she was in—Aunt Margery overflowing with happiness now that she had met her niece's fiancé, and Ben Maxwell looking at her—how? What were those grey eyes telling her? Was she imagining they were saying, 'Don't say anything to your aunt until I've had a chance to talk to you?'

She had read him accurately, it seemed, for he placed an arm about her, pulling her nearer to him. For one terrifying moment as his head came nearer, Tiffany thought he was going to kiss her, and she froze, numb at the thought. Then saw it was meant to look like a kiss from where her aunt was standing and for a split second as Ben Maxwell's mouth hovered above her own, she thought she saw a gleam of pure satisfaction in his eyes as he read her fear, then his mouth moved to her ear and she heard the grating whisper, 'Keep quiet until I see you later—and call me Ben.'

Then with a hand beneath an elbow of both Tiffany

and Margery Bradburn, he was escorting them to Tiffany's
Mini, her aunt telling him she was looking forward to
seeing him again.

'We'll have to see what we can arrange, Mrs Bradburn,'
he said non-committally as he satisfied himself that she
was comfortably seated before closing the door and going
round to the driver's side.

Tiffany looked at him helplessly, pleased her aunt
could not see the expression on his face. The kindness
thing that could be said for his look was that it was grim,
but for the sake of appearances she did as he had bidden
her and managed a husky ''Bye, B-Ben.' He stepped back
without a word, and Tiffany put the car into gear, then
sped out of the car park.

CHAPTER TWO

MARGERY BRADBURN was full of the man they had just
left in the car park, telling Tiffany she had told him she
lived away from London and he had asked her how long
she was staying. '... but as I told your wonderful fiancé
...' Oh God, Tiffany silently groaned, '... I came to
London on a trip with the W.I., and have to catch the
coach back at five o'clock.'

There were so many questions Tiffany wanted to ask,
but she would have to be very tactful. For some reason
Ben Maxwell didn't want her to confess to her aunt, and if
she was honest with herself, she was rather glad about that.
She knew she was being a moral 'coward, but she just
couldn't take that glow of sheer bliss from her aunt's face
—not just yet.

'How did you get to the airport, Aunty?' she asked.

Mrs Bradburn was happy to explain. 'I took a taxi—a bit extravagant, I know. You said on your card—thank you very much for that, by the way, dear—on your card you said you were coming home today, so I thought I would come along and give you a surprise.'

Darling aunt, you certainly did that, Tiffany thought. 'Er—so you met B-Ben accidentally while you were waiting for me?' She had heard of stranger coincidences, but could have done without this one.

'Oh no—I was a bit early getting there, so while I was waiting for you I went and asked the girl at the enquiry desk if Mr Ben Maxwell was in the building, and she told me he was expected some time after twelve.'

'They told you what time Mr ... Ben was coming in?' Tiffany asked faintly.

'Well, only after I told them I was a relative. Well,' she went on, 'I am nearly, aren't I?'

What could she answer to that? Her aunt had been to the airport several times over the past three years, so she would know how to get to the car park to see her. Tiffany only hoped her aunt hadn't mentioned the name Tiffany Nicholls in the same breath as Ben Maxwell's, or she would never live it down.

'So you waited for B-Ben and introduced yourself?' she asked unsteadily.

'Yes,' her aunt admitted happily. 'The girl I spoke with took me and showed me where to wait for him—I think he's such a nice man.'

'He—er—he didn't think it odd at all?' Tiffany just had to ask.

'Odd, dear? Why? Oh, you mean my turning up at the airport without him knowing I was coming?' Margery Bradburn considered for a moment or two before going

on. 'Now you come to mention it, he did look a little surprised, but then I don't suppose he expected to see me
there without you. He was very kind, though, when I
explained who I was—he asked me if I would like to have
lunch. Naturally he wanted me to tell him more about
you, but as I told him, "You'll have lots of time to hear
all Tiffany's little secrets".' Tiffany stifled another groan
and her aunt rattled serenely on. 'Anyway, I was getting
anxious by that time in case I missed seeing you, so Mr
Maxwell went and found out your plane had landed and
that you wouldn't be very long, and then he suggested
we go and sit in his car in the car park so we would be
sure not to miss you.'

It was impossible for Tiffany to concentrate on her
driving, take in all her aunt was saying, and sort out the
problem of Ben Maxwell's involvement at the same time.
She gave it up and concentrated on her driving.

Arriving at her flat, she insisted her aunt sit down
while she went into the kitchen to make a meal for them
both. Once alone, her mind flew off at a tangent. No
good blaming Aunt Margery, poor love, she was so pleased
with life at the moment, and she couldn't blame her for
introducing herself to Ben Maxwell, not after what she had
led her to believe. No, any blame attached to this whole
miserable business could be laid squarely at the door of
Tiffany Nicholls.

If only she hadn't given her aunt his name. If only ...
oh, what was the good? Too late now, it was done, and Aunt
Margery had always been so very good to her, she just
couldn't find it in her heart to disillusion her. She remembered the present she had brought her back from India,
but was so swamped by guilt she knew she would have to
give it to her another time. Tiffany leant her head against

the coolness of the kitchen wall. Her head was thundering all she needed was a headache.

Mrs Bradburn left just before four. Tiffany wanted to drive her to the coach, but her aunt said she rather liked the idea of riding in a London taxi, so Tiffany gave in and rang the taxi service for her, promising to go down to Middledeane as soon as she could.

'I shall expect you when I see you,' Margery Bradburn had twinkled back at her. 'I can't see you leaving Ben in London by himself,' and then to prove she was really with it, added, 'He is rather dishy, isn't he?' Tiffany had to grin at her, but somehow she had never thought of Ben Maxwell as being dishy.

She sat deep in thought for some time after her aunt had gone. It had been pure blind panic in case Aunt Margery had discovered her romance with Nick was off and started giving her another lecture on marriage that had led her into this situation. But she couldn't see Ben Maxwell taking that as an excuse. There was nothing for it, she would have to apologise to him, and take what was coming. She had felt some of his wrath before, and knew she was in for a none too pleasant time.

She recalled flying with Ben Maxwell on a similar trip to the one she had just finished, remembered how he prefered to have his meal after the co-pilot had eaten. Clive Winters had been the co-pilot, a married man, but with a weakness for a pretty face. Clive had flirted outrageously with her and rather than get him further into the bad books of Ben Maxwell, who by then was looking quite murderous, she had taken his slightly suggestive remarks without comment, secretly hoping she wouldn't be called to the flight deck too often. Ben Maxwell had obviously thought she was encouraging Clive, for he had given her a withering look, which she felt was undeserved, and when she had taken him his meal, his anger had almost reduced her to tears.

His quiet, 'How long have you been flying with Coronet?' should have warned her, but she had answered quite innocently.

'Nearly two years.'

'Then it's about time you knew that pilot and co-pilot do not, repeat *not*, eat identical meals.'

Of course she knew, it was one of the many rules of the Airline, a rule made so that in the unlikely event of something in one of the meals being contaminated, then there would still be one pilot fit to fly should the other go down with food poisoning. Any other captain would have laughed it off, but Ben Maxwell had made such an issue of it, she had gone back to the galley with her face scarlet, her knees quaking. It didn't make her feel any better when after bracing herself she had returned to the flight deck and found Clive Winters looking very subdued, making it obvious he too had been sorted out. That Clive was more restrained with her after that was little comfort to her wounded pride.

That had happened over twelve months ago and whenever she had flown with Ben Maxwell after that, something always seemed to happen to make her look inefficient, which was upsetting because she knew she was good at her job, and this had been borne out by the reports put in of her from other captains.

Tiffany took a couple of aspirins to relieve her spinning head, changed her uniform for a housecoat, and went and stretched out on her bed. Within minutes she was asleep.

When she awoke her headache had disappeared. That was a blessing anyway, though her thinking was no clearer. Ben Maxwell had said something about dinner, had said he would see her later. She didn't doubt that some time in the very near future she would be hanged, drawn and quartered by him, but thought even so it was unlikely he would call at her flat, though he would have no trouble in getting her address from Admin.

Automatically she bathed and donned fresh underwear, but on other occasions when anticipating she would be spending the evening alone she would normally have pulled on jeans and a sweater, she turned to her wardrobe and took out a dress.

When the knock sounded at the door, Tiffany shot to her feet, hoping against hope it would be Janet. Her hopes were doomed as she pulled the door open and saw the large frame of Ben Maxwell standing there, and for a few unspeaking seconds she was unable to utter one word as he stood regarding her. Her scant confidence rapidly disappeared beneath his all-encompassing gaze. She knew her full-length brown jersey dress showed off her shapely figure to advantage, the style making her look tall and aloof, its high collar embroidered in cream and a lighter shade of brown fitting closely around her elegant neck, but the courage her appearance had given her earlier vanished as she looked into hard grey eyes.

'C-come in, Mr Maxwell,' she stammered, stepping back to allow him to walk into her sitting room. The door closed, she made an attempt to gather her scattered wits together. 'Do sit down. W-would you like a drink?'

Ben Maxwell refused her offer of a drink and after waiting for her to be seated, took the chair facing her. 'Did your aunt get off all right?'

Her, 'Yes, thank you,' was greeted with silence. The palms of her hands were moist, and she found herself babbling about her aunt preferring to go to the coach by taxi, and pulled up short. 'Yes,' she said again, more slowly this time. 'I expect she'll be home soon.'

She darted him a quick look. He had no need to feel nervous, of course, and seemed in no way uncomfortable to be sitting opposite her, while she she was shaking like a leaf. She looked hurriedly away from him, unable to hold that straight look his grey eyes were giving her. She could feel the tension mounting, and it was obvious he had no intention of making it easy for her. In sheer desperation she plunged in at the deep end, her voice sounding thin and staccato in her ears.

'Mr Maxwell, I ... I know you c-can't possibly forgive me, but I am truly sorry about what h-happened today.' She paused, taking a deep breath in the unbearable silence and wishing he would say something, anything. But no, he was perfectly content to leave her to stammer out her excuses.

In that moment Tiffany felt she hated him. Sitting here in her home, his face impassive as he listened to her struggling to get her words out, waiting unspeaking for her to reveal 'all' as it were. Sitting there opposite her like a judge waiting to pass sentence. And suddenly she was angry. Who did he think he was? Agreed, he had a right to be sore, but he had no right at all to make her feel like a jibbering mass of jelly. Abruptly she stood up and saw he had risen too, she found him much too close for comfort and half turned away from him, anger making her voice sound tight and short.

'Mr Maxwell, I can do no more than apologise. My aunt truly believed we were en-engaged when she approached you.'

For the first time in what seemed an age, Ben Maxwell spoke, and Tiffany didn't care at all for his cool sardonic tones as he said :

'I wonder what gave Mrs Bradburn that most unlikely idea.'

Scarlet-cheeked, Tiffany couldn't look at him. 'I'm afraid I told her y-you were my fiancé.'

Ben Maxwell's voice came again, and this time the sarcasm fairly dripped from him. 'Forgive me if I appear to be a little absentminded, Miss Nicholls, but for the life of me I can't recall proposing to you.' His tone was harshly cutting as he went on, 'To be quite candid with you, I can't recall even *thinking* of asking you to be my wife.'

They had always pulled at opposite ends to each other and at his unconcealed sarcasm, Tiffany knew they had come from a just-beneath-the-surface dislike of each other into open warfare. But where his anger was ice-cold, hers was hot with fury. She had apologised, and it was obvious he was not going to accept her apology, but she'd see him in hell before she would grovel in front of him.

Tilting her chin slightly, she moved past him. 'I owed you an apology, Mr Maxwell,' she said stiffly, making for the door to intimate she would show him out. 'I have given you your apology, now ...'

'Not so fast, Nicholls.' The ice in his voice cut through her, shocked her into turning round. 'It isn't as simple as that.'

'Isn't as simple?' she repeated, not knowing what he was getting at, but her attention arrested when she longed for him to be gone.

'By now,' he elucidated, 'it will be all over Coronet Airlines that you and I are engaged—and I refuse to be made to look a fool by you or anyone else.'

Never had Tiffany heard such a tone in a man's voice. It was positively unarguable with, and bit into her with chill foreboding. She swallowed a lump in her throat.

'But no one else knows except the three of us,' she protested, not wanting to believe what he was saying, but unable to be sure her aunt hadn't talked to anyone else at Coronet.

'Allow me to enlighten you,' he said shortly. 'Sheila Roberts was standing barely a few yards from me, her ears at their usual coarse pitch, when Mrs Bradburn acc-introduced herself to me.' Tiffany knew he had been about to say 'accosted', but his choice of words wasn't all that important to her then.

Oh lord, what had she started? Wasn't it just her luck that Sheila Roberts, the Airline's chief gossipmonger, had heard her aunt in conversation with Ben Maxwell! As he said, it would be all over Coronet Airlines by now. Small wonder he was acting so brutishly. She raised troubled eyes to his and found to her surprise that although there was still a hard glint in his expression, the ice was disappearing as he studied her defeated look.

In an instant he made up his mind about something. 'I'm hungry. Get your coat, we'll resolve this problem over dinner.'

Tiffany wanted to refuse his command, for he did not ask, but commanded her to have dinner with him, but since something would have to be sorted out about this unholy mess, she found herself almost without knowing it donning her coat, turning her gas fire low, and sitting beside him as he guided his car through the London traffic.

He took her to a quiet, secluded hotel outside London. Tiffany had been out to dinner quite often in the three years since she had moved away from Middledeane, but she had been unaware that this place existed. By modern standards it was not a large hotel—perhaps that was part of its charm. It stood in its own grounds and the gardens were softly illuminated in the chill December evening, the lights making the greens of shrubs and bushes soft and muted and a perfect complement to the old stone brick-work of the hotel's façade.

Tiffany declined Ben Maxwell's offer of a pre-dinner drink, hoping that once he had some food inside him it might mellow him, and he guided her through to a small and pleasant dining room, which, because the first rush had gone, they had almost to themselves.

Ben Maxwell puzzled her. He was behaving very well even though she knew he was quietly furious with her and the position she had placed him in. She had expected him to ignore her until they got down to discussing their 'engagement'. But he hadn't ignored her—true, he hadn't been very forthcoming either—but she couldn't fault his manners. It was then she realised that Ben Maxwell had an inbred courtesy, and while aboard an aircraft or in the privacy of her home he could slate her, while she was out with him and in view of any outsider who might overhear, he would treat her in no way that would shame her in public view. She began to relax and even began to enjoy her meal too as it came to her that she was also hungry. The dining room was almost empty when his words reached her:

'Perhaps you would like to tell me how I came to be engaged to you?'

Ben Maxwell's smoothly asked question effectively made her appetite disappear. She made a show of emptying a piece of steak down her throat before answering him, wondering just how much she could get away with telling him. If, as she suspected, he wouldn't let her off without her telling the truth, then she knew she was going to be very red-faced at the end of it.

'Mr Maxwell,' she began.

'The name's Ben,' he reminded her. Idiotically, it also

reminded her she had been in his arms the last time he had told her to call him by his first name, and more idiotically, she found she was blushing at the memory. Her blush was witnessed by the hard man sitting across the table from her, and looking at him, she could have sworn her sudden colour had jolted him, for all his face remained as stern as ever.

'Ben,' she began again. Where to start? She just couldn't tell him about Nick—— Good heavens, she thought, amazed, she'd scarcely thought of Nick since she had seen her aunt and Ben Maxwell with each other today. She recovered herself quickly, and began, haltingly at first, to tell him just a small part of her aunt's attitude to marriage, and to herself in particular.

'I went to live with my aunt when my parents were divorced,' she told him, and trying not to be disloyal to her aunt, 'I love her very much and Aunt Margery only wants my happiness, I know—but because of the way my parents went about their marriage,' she had no intention of telling him anything of the bruising bewilderment with which she had witnessed her parents' constant rowing, 'well, because Aunt Margery thinks I've been put off marriage for life, she—she's—er—rather anxious about me.' Tiffany came to a halt, unable to read what the cold man opposite her was making of what she was telling him.

Ben Maxwell seemed, she thought, to have caught on to what she was saying, but his face remained expressionless, so she could tell nothing of what he was thinking. Then his voice came coldly to her, and as she had suspected, he had no intention of making it easy for her.

'Am I to believe,' he asked, as if he couldn't quite credit the conclusions of his summing up, 'that you told your aunt you were engaged to me purely to keep her happy—just because ...'

'It wasn't like that,' Tiffany broke in quickly before he could get warmed up to flatten her with his tongue. She effectively caused him to halt whatever else he was going to say, and she looked at him to see he was waiting, not too patiently either, for her to tell him if it wasn't like that, then exactly how it was. She looked away, unable to hold the straight look he was giving her. 'I ... I'd been going out with some—someone. Going steady, I thought——' She looked down at the tablecloth without seeing it, then struggled on. 'I thought he l-loved me, and ...' she got the strength from somewhere to return her eyes back to Ben Maxwell, who seemed to be listening more patiently now. 'And—well, yes, I did think it would make my aunt happy to know, and—— Oh, I know I should be ashamed of myself, but at the time I couldn't see anything wrong in her knowing.' Tiffany was beginning to feel disloyal to her wonderful aunt, and her voice faded out as she ended lamely, 'I thought—without conscious thought, if you know what I mean—that as well as making my aunt happy, it would—it would ...'

'It would stop her from getting on to you about marriage if you told her.'

'Yes, I suppose so.' Tiffany was feeling quite wretched now, her eyes again looking unseeingly down at the table-cloth. 'Only before I could get up the courage to tell her Nick and I were through, she was on the phone asking if he'd proposed, asking what his name was, and if he flew and ... and without thinking I'd told her he had proposed—then, probably because you were still fresh in my mind,' she coloured at that not wanting to remind him, but feeling the need to explain that Ben Maxwell wasn't always in her thoughts. 'You'd had a go at me shortly before,' she reminded him, her colour high, confessing, 'I was still pretty mad about it, and not wanting to give my aunt N-Nick's name, I gave her the first name that came into my head.'

There was a terse silence coming from across the table, and Tiffany had never felt so uncomfortable in her life. She had told Ben Maxwell everything—well, all he had a right to know—and sat there waiting for the biting indictment of her she knew he was capable of. It shook her to hear his voice sounding quite mild, as he asked:

'And what will you tell your aunt when you make it up with this Nick? That you fell rapidly out of love with Ben Maxwell—that you ...'

'I shan't be making it up with Nick,' Tiffany put in quickly. Then more slowly and bleakly, 'That's all finished.'

'Finished?' He sounded as if he didn't believe it. 'You'll rush straight into his arms the minute he calls,' he stated, making no bones about the fact he didn't believe her.

'I won't,' Tiffany returned, her face towards him, her eyes cold, her expression stony. 'Nick Cowley and I are through. If he came and begged me to go out with him I wouldn't.'

'He must have blotted his copybook with a vengeance,' Ben Maxwell said, holding her eyes steadily. 'What did he do to make him fall off the pedestal you'd placed him on?'

He was back to being his sweet, unlovable, sarcastic self, she thought, and since nothing was going to get her to reveal her own naïvety at what Nick had planned for that weekend, she returned Ben Maxwell's look coldly, and stared without emotion, 'That, Mr Maxwell, is none of your business.' She saw his jaw harden at that, and felt a fluttery sensation in the region of her stomach as with foreboding she realised one just didn't tell people like Ben Maxwell to mind their own business. She flicked her eyes away from him, glancing round the dining room and noting absently that they were the only people there now.

'Allow me to put you straight on a few matters, Tiffany

Nicholls,' he grated cuttingly, bringing her attention sharply back to him. 'I came off duty today looking forward to nothing more than enjoying a few days off, am accosted, in a place where the conversation can be overheard and relayed to all and sundry, and find myself having a girl thrust on me as my fiancée—a girl, I might add, who has the power to rub me up the wrong way quicker than anybody else I know.' Tiffany tried hard to hide a swallow of nervousness at that, but if Ben Maxwell noticed it it had no effect on him, for he went remorselessly on, every word biting into her. 'I objected strongly to having you thrust on me, but out of consideration for Mrs Bradburn, whom I judged to be one of nature's gentle people, I didn't give you away. I thought I would wait first to hear your explanation—wait for the explanation I'd thought must be a matter of life or death to have driven you to tell Mrs Bradburn that I'm the man you're going to marry.'

Tiffany's colour faded the more as Ben Maxwell continued to slate her, making it obvious their dislike of each other was mutual—but worse was to come, he hadn't finished with her yet. 'I've sat having dinner with you tonight, waited until I thought you were relaxed enough to tell me what had driven you to make such a wild claim, and have learned, to my disgust, that the only reason for your action was pure and utter cowardice, cowardice because you hadn't got the guts to tell your aunt you say you think so much of that your romance is off.' Tiffany winced at that, but Ben Maxwell went on without sparing her, telling her in a voice that lost none of its ice, 'After listening to you it crossed my mind to ignore the instinct that told me you must tell your aunt the engagement is off. I even gave thought to letting the engagement stand—even considered the possibility that we might play it along for a while. For that reason, and that reason only, I wanted to be sure your

ex-lover wouldn't come creeping back on the scene, and
for that reason alone I wanted to know what had gone
wrong between you so that I could judge for myself the
chances of his coming back into your life and so compli-
cate the issue further.' He was enunciating every word
clearly, and Tiffany didn't dare look at him as his remaining
words seared right through her. 'And you have the *audacity*
to tell me it's none of my business!'

Tiffany would dearly loved to have run away from him.
She had suffered from his tongue before, but never like this.
Their meal was over, there was nothing further to say,
nothing she could add that would make him feel any better
about her. She thought he was waiting for her to say
something, but what could she say? He'd had a right to
trounce her. He had been right to call her a coward—even
now, still quaking from his near-annihilation of her, she
still didn't know where she was going to get the courage
to tell her aunt what she knew had to be told. Since there
were no words coming from her, Ben Maxwell stood up
to indicate he too had nothing further to say, and silently
Tiffany went with him out to his car.

They had been driving for some minutes, with each
second becoming more unbearable than the last, when
Tiffany knew she owed him an apology. He was right in
the middle of this whole mess and it was she who had put
him there. But with him being so downright forbidding,
he was making that apology difficult to put into words.

'I ... I'm sorry I as good as told you to mind your own
business,' she got out after a faulty start. Her apology was
met with silence. But coward though she might be when
it came to hurting her aunt, her courage was not lacking in
any other direction. 'I didn't realise what you had in mind,'
she began again, 'w-why you wanted to know about Nick
and me.' She ploughed on, the pain of her words making

her voice husky. 'I suppose it—it still hurts to talk about it—that's why I couldn't tell you.'

Ben Maxwell's eyes left the road in front, and he turned to give her a brief look, his only indication that he had heard any of what she was saying before he returned his attention back to his driving.

'You're in love with him still?'

That she had to pause to think, am I still in love with Nick? jolted her. I'm too confused to know anything any more, she thought, when no answer came through to that question. When she didn't answer, Ben Maxwell must, she thought, have taken her silence for confirmation that she was still in love with Nick Cowley.

'You said earlier you thought he loved you—do I take it he doesn't any longer?'

'I don't think he ever did,' Tiffany said half to herself. Then realising that in the darkness of the car she could talk to Ben Maxwell and not be put off by any of the hard expressions she had witnessed in his face while they had been dining, 'Oh, he said he did, often, only—only I didn't know he was only saying it because ...' her voice tailed off. Ben Maxwell wouldn't be interested in any of that, besides which he was now drawing up outside the house where she had her apartment.

The car came to a halt, but before she could move, Ben Maxwell turned to her. 'Because?' he prompted.

She was glad of the darkness, it concealed her suddenly high colour. 'Oh, you know what men are,' she said, a feeling of irritation creeping over her because she knew she was very close to telling him what she was determined he should not know.

'I know what men are,' he agreed. 'But by the sound of it, you're trying to tell me you've only just found out.'

His tone niggled her. It told her clearly he thought she

knew all about men, and then some. 'How's this for your second surprise of the day?' she said, adopting an I-couldn't-care-less attitude. 'Tiffany Nicholls is so green that when a man tells her he loves her she's crass enough to think he means it—crass enough to think a declaration of love is naturally followed by the sound of wedding bells.'

'Stop trying to sound cynical,' Ben Maxwell's voice stopped her when she would have gone on. 'It doesn't suit you.' Then following up on what she had just told him, 'So this fellow told you he loved you, and when the first flush of romance had gone he ejected you out of his bed and out of his life?'

'I was never in his bed!' Tiffany shot back, too angry at his interpretation of her affair with Nick to think calmly.

'Never?' his tone was disbelieving.

'Never,' Tiffany confirmed more slowly.

'But you are in love with him—I thought bed was the natural sequence of events these days.'

'Not for everybody it isn't.' She could feel her temper beginning to slip and welcomed it; she was beginning to regret having ever apologised to him.

'You're different, are you?' He didn't sound as though he placed any credence in the truth of that. 'Tell me, would your not going to bed with this Nick Cowley have anything to do with the reason for your splitting up?'

Since Ben Maxwell as good as knew what he had asked back there in the hotel, Tiffany saw little point in withholding the rest of it, and in a few short words she told him about the planned weekend with Nick in Wales she had been looking forward to, ending with, 'His idea of a fun weekend, I discovered almost too late, was vastly different from mine.'

'Good God!' seemed to be dragged from him. 'I never

thought a girl with your looks could be so innocent. I'll agree with you—you are green, aren't you?'

Feeling a gullible idiot, Tiffany could see no point in discussing it any further, and made to move from the car.

'Stay where you are,' she was commanded. 'We still haven't fully sorted out what to do about being engaged to each other yet.'

Tiffany subsided into her seat. She had forgotten for quite some time now that the whole purpose in Ben Maxwell taking her to dinner had been to decide what to do about it. About to open her mouth and say she would deny the rumours, would confess everything to her aunt, she found him speaking before she could frame the sentences.

'We'll let the engagement stand for a while,' he said decisively, and when she turned to stare at him it was to see the harshness gone from his face, either that or a trick of the interior light he had just switched on, but his voice was matter-of-fact as he continued, 'There's bound to be the odd remark here and there at Coronet, so just go along with it—it will soon fizzle out.'

'But ...' Tiffany wasn't sure she wanted to let it stand after all—she didn't want to tell her aunt she wasn't engaged either, but of the two suddenly the thought of being engaged to Ben Maxwell, even if only to save her face, had her feeling more disquiet than even the thought of confessing to her aunt held.

'No buts,' he said, going back to being her stern dinner companion again. 'I've told you nobody is going to make me look a fool—you, Tiffany Nicholls, are now engaged to me—deny it, and you'll regret it.'

CHAPTER THREE

TIFFANY was up early the following morning and began sprucing up her already tidy flat. She must take her uniform in to the cleaners today; being smart was part of her job, though it ran through a fortune in cleaners' bills. Had she really had the nerve to call Ben Maxwell 'Ben' last night? The whole evening seemed unreal this morning somehow. She couldn't quite connect the reserved girl she knew herself to be with the girl who last night had told the forbidding airline captain the more intimate details of her relationship with Nick.

She shrugged thoughts of Nick away knowing that thoughts in that direction would get her precisely no-where. She was sure this morning she was still in love with him, and put any doubts she'd had last night down to the fact that Ben Maxwell was enough to confuse anybody. She concentrated her thoughts on her engagement. As Ben Maxwell had intimated, it would be a nine-day wonder at the airport, and then something else would happen and take precedence and the engagement would be forgotten.

A knock sounded on her door. Surely not Ben Maxwell? Her heart began thudding madly for no accountable reason and she opened the door to find Mr West, her landlord, standing there.

'Good morning, Mr West,' she greeted the stooped elderly man while pulling herself up sharply. She would be a nervous wreck if she went to pieces like this every time a knock sounded. Ben Maxwell had no reason to call and she wasn't afraid of his sarcastic tongue in any case.

Realising Mr West was still standing she bade him sit down.

'Have you come about the sash cord I reported to the estate agents?' she asked. It hadn't been repaired in her absence.

'Afraid not, Miss Nicholls,' Mr West said regretfully, and began to look so uncomfortable that Tiffany just had to ask:

'Is something wrong?' She had never seen him like this in the two and a half years she had known him.

He cleared his throat, then said gruffly, 'Well, to tell you the truth, Miss Nicholls, I just can't spare the cash to have any more repairs done.' He cleared his throat again. 'I'm sorry to have to tell you this, but—I've got to sell the place.' He looked away from her look of incredulity. 'I'm sorry, my dear, but you'll have to find somewhere else to live.' And while Tiffany was still trying to grasp that in an already overcrowded city she was going to have to hunt for another place, he went on to explain that with the cost of the upkeep of old property and taxes being what they were, he was having a job keeping his head above water. So there was nothing for it but to sell and Morton's, the estate agents, had told him the property would sell better if it was empty.

'I wanted to tell all my tenants personally, though Morton's will be sending you a formal notice through the post,' he went on abstractedly. 'They have to do that according to some Rent Act or other.' Mindless of her own plight, Tiffany's heart went out to him; poor man, he looked worried to death. 'I'm sorry about it, Miss Nicholls,' he apologised, 'but you can see how I'm placed.'

Her household chores were forgotten after he had gone and the shock of his news began to fade. Getting other accommodation wasn't going to be easy, she'd only managed to get this flat because a fellow stewardess had tipped her off that she was leaving. She would have to start looking straight away. Being out of the country for weeks at a time made it extra difficult—— And what about Janet and Bill downstairs? How on earth were they going to find somewhere, especially with a three-year-old son? Miss Tucker too on the ground floor, she would have to find somewhere. Thinking of the other residents made Tiffany realise her worries were small compared with theirs. And without thinking further she left her flat and went and knocked on Janet's door.

'He's been to see you, then?' Janet said as Tiffany followed her into the kitchen. 'I'm just making some coffee —want some?'

'Please.'

Bill, Janet told her when they settled down, had been offered a job in Manchester by the firm he worked for. 'We've been thinking about it for a couple of days now, so I expect this will decide things for us, especially as they'd said they'll help us with accommodation. Of course Bill doesn't know yet that we've had our marching orders, so I shall have to see what he thinks.'

They chatted on for a while longer, Janet saying that rented places were snaffled up before they ever got on to estate agents' books, and flats advertised in the paper were taken before the printer's ink was dry. It was a depressing outlook.

'What about Miss Tucker?' Tiffany asked. 'She's been here years, hasn't she?'

'She was here before we came, and we've been here seven years. But I expect she'll go and live with her sister on the coast. I know she'd been thinking about it, she was telling me so the other day.'

It looks very much as though I shall be the only one on

the flat-hunting trail, Tiffany thought, and with Janet's help she searched through the paper.

The days remaining before her next flight were spent flat-hunting, but it was hopeless. She was out early, following up adverts in the paper, adverts in shop windows, trudging from estate to estate agent, and even put her own ad. in the paper, but so far no replies.

The day before she was due to go back on duty Tiffany rang her aunt apologising for not ringing before and explaining what had happened. She had received her notice to quit from Morton's and her rent was paid quarterly in advance, so she had three months in which to find alternative accommodation.

'How's Ben?' queried Margery Bradburn, completely igoring Tiffany's anguish at the thought of being homeless.

'Ben?—Oh, Ben's fine.'

'Such a nice man. I'm so pleased for you, Tiffany.'

It just wasn't getting through to Aunt Margery, thought Tiffany, that her mind was more on finding somewhere to live than on Ben Maxwell. She gave up trying in the end and listened instead to her aunt going on for a full five minutes singing the praises of Ben and what a lucky girl she was, and enquiring when the wedding was to be.

Taken up as her off-duty period had been with her desperate search for accommodation, the fact that she was now engaged, and to whom, had taken a back seat in Tiffany's thoughts. But her first day back on duty she was met with comments such as 'Dark horse!' and 'How did you manage it, Tiffany?' and the remembrance that everyone knew she was engaged to Ben was brought fully to the forefront of her mind by overhearing Sheila Roberts saying to one of the other stewardesses, 'I've been angling for Ben Maxwell ever since I first clapped eyes on him.' She missed what was being said next as she clattered purposefully in the galley, only to stop and hear Sheila saying, ' . . . so all that cold shoulder treatment they gave each other was pure camouflage.' The fact that she and Ben were nearly always at daggers drawn had not gone unnoticed, then.

Tiffany visited many foreign countries in the next six weeks. Her rest days back in England had been spent in hunting for a flat, only to leave her more and more depressed at not being able to find anything. The teasing about her and Ben Maxwell had now died down, their engagement was now accepted and rarely referred to.

She let herself into her flat, dumped her case down on the floor, and reflected that life was going to be very dull until her engagement 'fizzled out'. Peter Clarke, the navigator on the run she had just finished, had asked her out when they landed in Cape Town, and on the point of accepting, for Peter was good fun in a harmless way, she had found his invitation immediately withdrawn as he had remembered, 'I'm sorry, Tiffany—I forgot you were engaged.'

She hadn't given a thought to that side of her engagement, and paused to consider that since most of the men she knew knew Ben also, should some of the less principled ask her out, how in fairness to Ben could she accept? It wouldn't be fair to accept invitations out from any of the men they weren't mutually acquainted with either, she saw, and suddenly she was fed up. Nothing was going right.

She moved further into the sitting room, got no further than undoing the top two buttons of her jacket, when her phone rang. Straightaway she recognised Ben Maxwell's voice, deep and masculine, coming across to her over the wires.

'Tiffany?'

'Yes.' She wondered what he wanted. She had enough on her plate without hearing any of his acid.

'Ben Maxwell.' She already knew that—he didn't sound in a very good humour. 'I want to see you—I'll come round.'

Typical Ben Maxwell, Tiffany thought as she banged the receiver back on its rest. No 'Please may I?' No 'Is it convenient?' Just, 'I want to see you—I'll come round'.

Forgoing the luxury of the bath she had been looking forward to, Tiffany washed and changed into a denim shirt and jeans, and just had time to add a touch of lipstick, then Ben Maxwell was there.

He hadn't wasted any time, she thought as she let him into her sitting room; he looked ill-humoured as he had sounded on the phone, was as big as she remembered him, and seemed to fill her tiny flat as he followed her in. Then cutting short her look of enquiry as to why he wanted to see her, he seemed to notice that if she had thought he wasn't in the best of humours—he could see she was looking decidedly fed up herself.

'What's wrong?'

His short enquiry made her realise her face must be very expressive if he had read there the depression she was feeling. 'What's right?' she answered belligerently, and saw from the way his eyes narrowed that he didn't take very kindly to her tone. She felt his steady gaze on her and knew if she didn't do something to save the situation they would both be firing broadsides at each other uncaring where they landed. 'Everything's wrong,' she confessed, hating herself for backing down under the growing anger she saw creeping into his eyes. If he threw a sarcastic 'We all have our problems' regardless of who he was and the fact that he could make life difficult for her the next time she flew with him, Tiffany knew her own temper would get out

of control and she would order him from her flat—whether
he went or not was another matter.

When he spoke his tone was quite mild, which effectively
sent her rising temper down a few degrees. 'Care to tell
me what's troubling you?'

Ben Maxwell was the last person Tiffany would have
thought of as her confidant, but since he already knew so
much about her, she sat down and he followed suit, and
she found herself telling him, 'Well, for one thing this
house is being sold, so I have to find somewhere else to
live—it's next to impossible to find anywhere to rent,
and my rest days are spent traipsing around looking for
another apartment . . .'

'Hopeless, is it?' he enquired, his eyes looking thoughtful.

'You've said it,' Tiffany acknowledged. 'It's hopeless.'

'You intimated there's more than one thing bothering
you,' he said shrewdly. 'What else is getting you down?'

'Everything comes at once, doesn't it?' Tiffany shrugged,
trying to lighten the atmosphere and not succeeding very
well. She felt low, and trying not to let him see how really
down she was didn't help to lift her any. Then with a
feeling, unfairly, she realised later, that half her problems
were his fault anyway, she fully unburdened herself.

'When I've finished trudging the rounds of estate agents
and possible leads, I find I have no social life.'

'No social life?' he repeated disbelievingly. 'From what
I've seen you're popular with the opposite sex.'

She hadn't thought he'd even noticed. 'I was before I
became en-engaged,' she admitted, seeing no point in false
modesty, but faltering over the word engaged. 'But now
none of our mutual acquaintances invite me out because
they think I'm engaged to you—and . . . and I don't feel I

can go out with any of my non-airline male friends because that doesn't seem fair to you either.'

She caught him giving her a sharp look when she glanced across at him. 'You're a very honest fiancée, I must say, Tiffany. Not many girls would see our engagement that way.'

'Well, you wouldn't like it, would you?' she asked, hoping he would say he couldn't care less what she did in her off time and so give her carte blanche to do what she wanted. Patti Marshall was having another of her parties tonight, it might cheer her up to go there ...

'No, I wouldn't like it,' he agreed, and Tiffany went back to being fed up again. 'Anything else troubling you?' he enquired.

'Well, since you want to know the lot,' Tiffany began, her aggression rising to realise she might as well be living on a deserted isle for all the fun she was getting out of life at the moment, 'some time over the next few days I've got to ring Aunt Margery and let her know I've landed safely—she'll worry if I don't—and I know when I do she'll do nothing but sing your praises.' Her aggression disappeared, and her voice began to get all wobbly. 'I don't think I can take the question again of when you and I are going to get married,' she told him, ending, 'and ... and I'm f-fed up!'

Tiffany hated anyone to see her cry and struggled hard against the tears that threatened. Ben Maxwell hadn't moved and she was afraid to look at him, realising he must think her a proper little misery. Ousting her self-pity, she recalled he had come to her flat ten minutes ago not with the purpose of sitting listening to her tale of woe—why he had come she didn't know, but whatever his reason for calling, it couldn't make her feel any worse than she was right now. Feeling more in control of herself, she lifted her head and summoned up a small self-conscious smile.

'Sorry to be such a pain in the neck—I didn't mean to go on like that.'

He didn't smile back, and her own smile faded. She wished she'd never apologised in the first place. Her full control returned rapidly at the hard look on his face. She must have been an idiot to let go in front of him like that, he didn't care a button about how she was feeling— but then why should he?

'So much for my problems,' she finished, adopting a cool air. 'You didn't come here to listen to me. What did you come for, Mr Maxwell?'

By calling him Mr Maxwell she was able, she thought, to keep everything cool and businesslike between them. But when his hand dipped into his jacket pocket and without taking his narrowed eyes off her face, he withdrew the folded newspaper she had noticed jutting out when he had sat down, Tiffany had an uncanny premonition that disaster was about to strike. His face looked grim as he opened out the paper and without a word handed it over to her.

'What . . . ?' Tiffany questioned, her eyes going to the top of the paper to see which one it was. *Middledeane and Marchberrow Gazette,* she saw. 'But this is Aunt Margery's local newspaper,' she said, looking at him for enlightenment. 'Why . . .'

'Look at the announcement column,' he told her, then completely shattered her cool air. 'Under Engagements.'

Oh no, Tiffany thought, even before she found the page, saw there was only one engagement and read quickly, '. . . pleased to announce the engagement of Tiffany Margery Nicholls to Benedict Rowley-Maxwell, son of . . .' Tiffany groaned out loud. And she had thought nothing else could happen—this crowned the lot! But where did Aunt Margery get her information, she wondered with one part of her mind as she read on '... son of Mr and the late Mrs Harvey Rowley-Maxwell'. Afraid to look at him, Tiffany let the paper fall in her lap. Oh God, Aunt Margery —would this nightmare never end?

'I'm sorry, Ben—so sorry,' she said huskily. Then her lips firmed as she realised what she must do. He already thought she was a coward where her aunt was concerned, but this was too much. He had been more than accommodating in letting her use him the way she had, but he must by now be ready to explode—he hadn't asked to become involved. Tiffany's mind was made up. Aunt Margery was going to be upset, but the whole farce had to be stopped here and now. There was no knowing what Aunt Margery would do next in her innocence.

'I'll see a retraction goes in straight away,' she said firmly. 'I'll go down to Middledeane today and explain to my aunt exactly what I did.'

She heard Ben move, felt the shadow of him standing in front of her. 'I have a solution, Tiffany, and it's not a retraction.' Her head came up then, but where she had expected him to look at her as if ready to tear her apart, although unsmiling, she saw nothing in his face to make her afraid of what he would do. Then he came and sat beside her on the small two-seater settee and unconsciously Tiffany moved up to make room for him.

'Not a retraction?' she repeated, not knowing quite where she was any more. 'But ...'

'Just hear me out,' his voice stopped her when she would have argued that the only solution she could think of now was to be painfully honest with her aunt. 'I've said I have a solution,' Ben went on. 'But before I tell you what it is, and at the risk of making you even more upset, I think you should know exactly what your aunt has triggered off by putting this announcement in the paper.' Tiffany wanted to groan out loud again, but managed to stifle it—she had a feeling there was far worse to come. 'Have you heard of a Colonel Wainwright?' he asked.

She had, but didn't know what he had got to do with anything. 'The one I know lives in Marchberrow—he's a J.P., I think.'

'That's the one,' Ben confirmed. 'Well, it just so happens that Colonel Wainwright is a great friend of my father's—that being so, when Colonel Wainwright saw I'd got myself engaged,' he tapped the paper resting on the arm of the settee, 'he sent a copy of this paper to my father.'

All Tiffany's senses were screaming, oh no, was there no end to it? Ben carried on, ignoring the sudden whiteness of her face.

'Needless to say, my father wrote to me—a not very polite letter, I might add—asking if there was any particular reason why he should be the last to know.' Tiffany could see from where Ben got his sarcastic tongue. 'I should mention,' he continued, a flat note entering his voice, 'that my father has been in hospital in Switzerland for the past few months—not to underline it too heavily, he's more than a little sensitive at being cut off from the rest of the world.'

Tiffany felt she was going mad. All this had grown from that first senseless, impulsive lie—it was all down to her. She was ready to do anything, anything at all to show Ben how contrite she was.

'What do you want me to do?' she asked him, half turning on the settee, her eyes showing him she would stop at nothing to redress what she had done, and confirmed it by saying, 'I'll do anything—anything you ask.' There was no doubting her sincerity. But Ben Maxwell asked just the same:

'Are you sure about that?'

'Positive—just name it.'

She saw a glint come into his eyes, then his expression stern, he said, 'Come and live with me, Tiffany.'

Whatever she had expected, that was the last thing that had gone through her mind, and her face that had been white went scarlet, only to pale to ashen as she whispered, disbelieving her hearing, 'As ... as though we were m-married, do you mean?' before her senses set up an outraged clamouring, so that she could only just make out what else he was saying.

'By God, Tiffany, you're trusting,' he gritted harshly. 'I'd already decided the best way out of this mess was for us to be married.' She was receiving shock after shock, but Ben was so angry with her he didn't wait for his words to register, but went straight on. 'Don't you realise the serious trouble you could get yourself into telling a man you barely know that you'll do anything he asks? Thank your lucky stars, Tiffany Nicholls, that I have more regard for your innocence than to take you to live with me without the benefit of a wedding ring.' Tiffany's colour was high as he thundered to a stop.

And as what he was saying made itself comprehended on her scattered senses, she was on her feet saying, 'Married?' She felt completely floored. 'Are you saying you want us to be married?'

'You sound more shocked now than when you thought I was suggesting you live with me without the Church's blessing.' His voice was cool again now, and he stretched out a hand to pull her to sit beside him on the settee again.

'I wasn't—I ... I have no intention of living with you,

married or not,' she managed after a hesitant start.

'You said you would do anything,' he reminded her.

'Yes, but—marriage! It's ridiculous!'

She dared a look and saw he didn't share her opinion that it was ridiculous. She looked away, shaken to the very core. When she married it would be for love—she didn't think she even liked Ben Maxwell very much—and he was calmly sitting there, calmly waiting for her to agree—no, not even agree—acquiesce to his decision to marry her.

'I can't marry you,' she said bluntly. 'It's unthinkable. If this is your solution to the mess I've got us into, then I'm afraid I don't think much of it. All I have to do is to tell Aunt Margery what I've done,' her spirits quailed at the thought, but she went bravely on. 'M-my aunt will put a retraction in the paper and that will be the end of it.'

'Aren't you rather forgetting my part in all this?' His voice was icy, and Tiffany felt a shiver of apprehension run along her spine.

'I'm sorry, Ben—I truly am. If—If you'll let me have your father's address I'll write to him and explain everything to him.'

'No!' It was said sharply, and echoed round her flat, and he meant it. A tense silence followed and Tiffany's mouth set in a mutinous line until Ben spoke again, but this time the edge had gone from his voice and he looked ready to discuss the problem more amicably. 'I know you don't like me, Tiffany,' he said, and when her eyes swivelled to look at him conceding she had done very little to hide her feelings about him, he said, 'Oh yes—I've seen the dislike in your eyes every now and then—but whether we like each other or not doesn't come into it.' He was clearly telling her he didn't like her either, which made his suggestion of marriage even more preposterous. 'As I see it, being married to me would solve a lot of your problems.'

Tiffany still thought their getting married to each other too much of a drastic step to take. Of course it would take the pressure of Aunt Margery off her, and since Ben had said, 'Come and live with me' the problem of finding somewhere else to live would be solved. In telling him about her impending homelessness she had played straight into his hands, she could see that now—but one didn't get married solely for somewhere to live, even if one did have a streak of cowardice when it came to hurting a person as sweet as Aunt Margery.

'No, Ben,' she refused again, finding his name now rolled easily off her tongue. 'I can't even consider it.'

'Why not?'

He wasn't going to be easily put off, it seemed. 'Well, for one thing it's too one-sided—I mean—— Well, I know married to you I wouldn't have Aunt Margery pressuring me to get married, and . . . and you mentioned I'd be living with you so I wouldn't have the problem of finding somewhere to live—but what would you get out of it?' She stopped abruptly, a wave of furious colour washing her face. 'Oh,' she said, and felt herself break out in a cold sweat as Ben Maxwell looked at her steadily obviously finding no difficulty in following her line of thinking.

'It wasn't in my mind to marry you for the other benefits that go with being man and wife,' he told her coolly, letting her know without a doubt that Nick Cowley might be on fire to get her into bed with him, but as far as Ben Maxwell was concerned, Tiffany Nicholls left him cold in the sex department. Then in case it wasn't blindingly clear to her, he continued to leave her in no doubt whatsoever. 'You don't need to tell me you're attractive, a man would have to be blind not to see it—but quite honestly, Tiffany, making love to you doesn't come into my scheme of things.'

Her colour came again at his brutal honesty. He even gave her a look which she read as meaning she'd be the lucky one, not him, if she ever found herself on the receiving end of his favours.

'So,' she said, her chin coming up as she forced herself to face him, 'physically I leave you cold—all right, I accept that—but I still couldn't marry you.'

'Because it's too one-sided and you can't see what I would get out of it,' said Ben, and Tiffany's look confirmed. Then after a long pause, he breathed in deeply and said as though against his will, 'Very well, Tiffany—I can see you won't agree to marry me unless I level with you, so I'll confess it would suit me very well to be married right now.'

'You—er ...' Her surprise was holding her tonguetied. Speechlessly she looked at him and to her further surprise saw from his look that Ben Maxwell would rather tell her anything than the reason why it would suit him to be married.

'As I've told you,' he began slowly, 'my father is in hospital in Switzerland. About a year ago he married an ex-girl-friend of mine, and—well, to cut the story short,' he said gruffly, giving Tiffany the distinct impression that if she didn't know better she would have thought the great Ben Maxwell was embarrassed, 'the old goat seems to think we still have a shine for each other. It's nonsense, of course,' he went on, 'but the more Frances and I try to tell him there's nothing between us, the more convinced he becomes that there is. He should be home by now fully recovered, but worrying over a non-existent problem is holding back his progress.' He ended what he was telling her on a relieved kind of note, as if glad it was all said and out of the way. 'Now do you see why I need a wife? It wouldn't be all one-sided, Tiffany.'

Tiffany was dumbfounded, all her sympathy with his father in Switzerland—he must be pretty near demented so far away from his wife, away from the woman he loved, tormented by suspicion and jealousy.

'Oh, Ben—I'm so sorry about your father.'

Her momentary weakening was enough to give him the opening he had been waiting for. 'Look at it logically,' he told her. 'Our marriage needn't be a permanent one. Once my father is well again and your aunt is off her hobby-horse, we can have the marriage annulled.'

'Annulled?' Tiffany queried. He was going too fast for her to catch up with him.

'Annulment applies where a marriage has not been consummated,' he told her, and Tiffany flushed scarlet again. Then Ben was back to urging her to be logical, making it all sound so sane and sensible, so much so that she began to feel she was not thinking straight in even considering turning his proposition down. It did sound logical the way he put it, she had to admit, and yet ... 'You need somewhere to live,' he was saying. 'I have a spare bedroom in my flat doing nothing—I wouldn't object if you wanted to keep on with your job.'

'Of course I'd want to keep on with my job,' she came back without having to think about it.

'There you are, then—we would hardly ever see each other apart from occasionally bumping into each other when we weren't flying.'

It sounded the perfect solution for them both, but Tiffany didn't know. It didn't worry her that there was no romance in what he proposed, heaven forbid, she was still too sore from Nick Cowley to want to try romance again for a very long time to come, but there had to be a snag somewhere, though with Ben talking so logically, she couldn't see where.

'How about it, Tiffany?—it would help my father to get well again.'

Tiffany almost capitulated at that, but something held her back. 'I don't know—I just don't know. I . . . I need time to think.' She looked at him, and noticed for the first time how tired and drawn he looked. 'Have you just finished duty too?' she asked quietly.

'No. I've just come back from Switzerland.'

'You went to see your father after receiving his letter?' she questioned, not needing his confirmation.

'It was the least I could do.'

He didn't tell her what had passed between himself and his father, but she guessed from his expression that it hadn't been an easy meeting. At that moment she would dearly love to be able to tell him she would marry him, if only she could relay the message back to his father and so set him on the road to recovery, but she felt she was being pressganged into something she might later regret.

'I need time to think, Ben,' she reiterated.

He stood up; it seemed he had nothing else to say to her. But in that she was wrong. 'I'll give you until eight o'clock this evening,' he told her, and while she looked up at him wanting to argue that that wasn't nearly enough time, he walked to the door to turn and give her a long steady look. 'Have your mind made up one way or the other by then, Tiffany,' he instructed. He was back to being the commanding Ben Maxwell.

CHAPTER FOUR

How could she marry a man she didn't love? Would it really mean so much to Ben's father's recovery to have his son married? These thoughts bombarded Tiffany as she set about the routine jobs that awaited her each time she returned from a flight. How close had this Frances person been to Ben before she had thrown him over? Thrown him over? That couldn't be right ... He hadn't said she had thrown him over and if she thought about it she couldn't see *any* girl telling him to take a walk. He was a self-assured, experienced man, she couldn't see him ever being on the receiving end of a 'Dear John letter'. Was Frances still in love with him? Had she ever been in love with him? Tiffany gave it up—she was just going round and around in circles.

Mechanically she made herself a sandwich and a hot drink. She ought to ring Aunt Margery and let her know she was back, but much as she loved her, she couldn't face making the call yet.

Some time after seven Tiffany changed into a fresh pair of jeans and a clean sweater. She had been grubbing around cleaning and polishing earlier, but not knowing whether Ben would telephone or call personally at her flat she didn't want to change into anything dressy. It had been a long wearing day, but still too short for her to have to come to any sort of decision; her mind had been see-sawing backwards and forwards the whole time.

A minute after eight Ben arrived. Tiffany noticed that like herself, he was casually dressed—beige cavalry twill trousers with a fawn sweater showing beneath his sheepskin coat. He brought a breath of the January air with him and studied her face, seeming to read in that one look that she had no answer ready for him. He still had his car keys in his hand.

'Care to come for a spin?'

Tiffany nodded, on edge. 'I'll just get my jacket.' She wondered if he was feeling the same tension that held her in its grip, but could tell nothing from his expression.

She found the motion of the car relaxing. Ben was as good a driver as he was a pilot, and the further they drove the more her tension eased. The reason for his calling was not discussed and gradually, grateful to him for allowing her this time to herself, Tiffany warmed to her companion. She felt nearer to being at ease with him than she had ever been.

Then he drew up in front of a fairly new-looking block of apartments three stories high. 'Where are we?' she asked, sitting up and looking about her.

'My place,' he replied, and Tiffany felt her tension rushing in again. 'I could do with a cup of coffee——Come up and make it for me.'

Her heart began to thud as they ignored the elevator and climbed the two flights of stairs to his flat. Her hurried heartbeats had nothing at all to do with the exertion of climbing the stairs, she admitted, tension was tying her nerves into quivering, jerking knots.

His sitting room was a delight. Her first impression was of pale green walls and mahogany furniture, but as she began to look at the room, she realised it was the perfect blend of the old and the new that made it so attractive. Her hand rubbed along the smooth edge of his writing desk; it had a beautiful feel to it—the cost of the furnishings alone must have been colossal. Whatever must he have thought about her own home? she wondered. By comparison her flat, though clean and bright, must have appeared to him to be decidedly shabby. She could never live here, her decision was upon her without her knowing it. Ben's flat was too—too—what was the word she was searching for? Perfect, that was it, Ben's home was perfect—once living here she would never want to leave. She turned, unaware that he had been watching her, reading the expressions that had flitted across her face. Tiffany knew she had to tell him.

'Ben, I ...'

'I'm gasping for that coffee, Tiffany,' he interrupted, almost as if he knew she was about to tell him she couldn't marry him, she thought. He gave her a brief smile, but she noted the smile didn't reach his eyes.

He took her through a door that led into the kitchen, and left her to it. Never had she felt so tormented. She would make him his coffee, then ask him to ring for a taxi, and go. He certainly wouldn't want the job of an hour's run back to her flat after she had turned down his marriage proposal.

Absently her eyes glanced along the stainless steel sink unit, over the various other units and on to a tray holding sugar bowl and teapot. Then her eyes lighted on a tea-cosy, and as if hypnotised she stared at it. It had no place in this streamlined kitchen, for it was a woollen one, so exactly like her own, even to the moulting pom-pom on top. Tiffany stared hard, and still couldn't believe it. She blinked—it was still there.

Fleetingly she thought, how ridiculous to make up your mind to marry someone on seeing a homely-looking tea-cosy with a moulting pom-pom. It was a relief to feel the tension go out of her.

Her tension might have disappeared, but her hands were

shaking as she carried the tray into the sitting room. Ben rose from his chair and took the tray from her, and they both subsided into chairs as Tiffany handed him his coffee. If he saw her shaking hands, he didn't say anything but accepted his coffee had slopped over into his saucer without comment. Looking quickly at him Tiffany saw that while his eyes were alert, the rest of him was giving nothing away. She must tell him now, she thought, tell him before tension grew between them again.

Her voice was unsteady when it made itself heard.

'M-may I see my bedroom, please?'

For a split second his face showed no reaction that in a roundabout way she had agreed to marry him, then a slow, warm smile started to dawn in his eyes, travelled the length of his face, and settled in a broad grin at his mouth.

In that moment, Tiffany Nicholls fell in love with Ben Maxwell. Tiffany upset her coffee and looked down at the mess she had made and heard a roaring in her ears. One didn't faint with love, but it had been a near thing, she realised, as the roaring ceased and she looked at him again. He was still smiling, and she still loved him, and then she knew exactly why she had agreed to marry him. It had nothing to do with her aunt, or his father, for without her being aware of it her heart had told her she loved him, only her mind hadn't recognised the fact until he had smiled. Dimly she heard him say, 'I'll get a cloth,' and she was glad of those few minutes to be by herself.

How could she be in love with him? She was in love with Nick. Then Nick Cowley faded into the background; she had felt nothing for him when compared with this all-consuming feeling Ben Maxwell aroused in her.

Ben was very matter-of-fact when he returned, she could have imagined that grin, for there was nothing in his face to show that he was pleased she had agreed to marry him. But that smile was within him, she knew it was.

'I'll show you over the place,' he was telling her, while she was trying to keep what she felt for him well out of sight. 'Then we'll have some fresh coffee.'

He showed her the room which was to be hers first. The walls were a satiny grey colour she didn't care much for in a bedroom, but the rest of the room was as perfect as the sitting room and kitchen were, apart from that tea-cosy. Built-in wardrobes, a dressing table, a single bed and bedside table.

'If there's anything you would like added or taken out, tell me,' Ben instructed her. Tiffany told him everything was fine. No point in having the colour of the walls changed. She might not be here all that long.

They went from the room she was to use to the room next door. 'This is my room,' he said, stepping back to allow her to go in front of him. His room was masculine in every detail. Books on his bedside table, a reading light over the bed. His bed was a double one, she saw; he would need it too, she thought, looking at him and catching her breath at her new-found feeling for him. He was well over six feet tall and without any surplus fat, broad into the bargain. Her eyes slid down to where his hips tapered slimly, and she looked quickly away.

She felt her tension mounting again, and turning quickly left his bedroom, waiting for him to follow. He showed her the bathroom, complete with bath and shower—a shower was a luxury she didn't have in her small flat. There was no comparison between their two apartments anyway, except of course for that darling little tea-cosy.

It was Ben who made the second lot of coffee and once more seated in the sitting room, he asked, 'Do you want to be married from Middledeane?'

'Aunty will want me to.'

'Well, as it's through your aunt this whole thing got started, I suppose it's the least we can do.'

Tiffany went pink, and started to say, 'I'm sorry ...' before Ben cut her short.

'This marriage is to the advantage of both of us, Tiffany, so please stop apologising.' Glancing at his watch, he stood up. 'It's nearly midnight, so I suggest I take you home.' He paused, his voice sounding casual as though the thought had just come to him. 'You could sleep here if you like,' and at her startled expression. 'But you wouldn't do that, would you?'

Tiffany shook her head, finding a constriction in her throat preventing her from answering. She knew his offer was as straightforward as it sounded, and it would save him a two-hour drive to her flat and back. She watched and saw his face take on a tight look.

'You were prepared to sleep under the same roof as Nick Cowley, though, weren't you?'

'That was different,' she managed, and saw his jaw harden.

'Because you are in love with *him*?'

She swallowed, not sure why he was suddenly coming over all aggressive, but prepared to tell him anything other than the truth. 'Something like that,' she answered, her voice husky. Ben would never know the love she had felt for Nick was insignificant compared to this new emotion that had awakened in her.

On the way back to her flat, Ben told her since she would have to be out of her accommodation shortly, they would be married as soon as it could be arranged. 'I'll call for you early tomorrow morning,' he went on matter-of-factly, 'and we'll drive down to Middledeane, tell your aunt and see the vicar while we're there.'

Tiffany was unsure what she said in reply—everything

seemed to be moving so quickly, she felt she no longer had any control. Reaction was beginning to set in when he escorted her to the door of her flat, and she was beginning to feel not a little scared at what she had committed herself to. She tried to keep the panicky feeling from showing in her eyes, but with the door of her flat open, the light on, she turned to say goodnight to him, and found him looking down at her, his expression softening.

'Cold feet already?' There was a teasing note in his voice she hadn't expected him to have, but the half smile that accompanied his words made her feel a whole lot better.

'Just a bit,' she said, swallowing hard.

'It will be all right, Tiffany.' His hand came up and gave her arm a brief squeeze. 'Just trust me,' he added, then he was gone.

Tiffany spent a troubled night, and awoke to the clamouring of her alarm, her mind none the easier for a fitful few hours' sleep. Had she really told Ben she would marry him? Her heart turned over at the thought, and in the cold light of day she knew she must have taken leave of her senses last night. Why, she barely knew him, how could she ever have contemplated doing such a thing? No amount of coercion from Aunt Margery was worth taking such a step. Her heart missed a beat as she realised she would have to tell Ben this morning that she couldn't go through with it.

As soon as she saw him in her doorway, Tiffany knew the love for him that had come to her unasked was still with her, making it impossible to get the carefully prepared words out.

'Have you telephoned Mrs Bradburn to let her know to expect us?' he asked after a perfunctory greeting.

'I ... I thought we'd surprise her,' she made up on the

spur of the moment, while her senses screamed, 'Tell
him—Tell him you aren't going to marry him—Tell him
before he takes you down to his car'. But no words came,
and they were both silent as the car nosed its way to
Middledeane.

Once they had left London behind Ben began to make
casual conversation and as some of his remarks required
an answer, very soon Tiffany found herself in easy conversation with him, and gradually the panicky feeling that
had threatened to overwhelm her since she had first opened
her eyes that morning began to dwindle, and the further
they motored on, she began to realise with wonder that
she was actually enjoying his company, realised too that
if it hadn't been for her shattering discovery that she loved
him, she would have told him this morning she had
changed her mind—it all seemed so fantastic—and yet,
since she did love him, she couldn't help wanting some
short time as his wife.

Perhaps it was going to be all right. It *would* be all right,
she vowed as all thoughts of telling him she couldn't marry
him disappeared. Ben needed her help for his father's sake,
and apart from her accommodation problem, she needed
Ben's help, sorry though she was to admit it, she needed
his help to give her some peace from Aunt Margery, for
as dear as she was, Aunt Margery was slowly wearing her
down.

It would be all right, Tiffany kept repeating, and took a
sideways look at the man she had promised to marry.
Aware of her glance on him, Ben turned his head to look at
her, and as if knowing what she was thinking, gave her a
reassuring half smile. Tiffany's stomach flipped, and she
turned to stare out of the window, frightened to smile back
in case he read more of her thoughts and discovered
exactly how his smile affected her.

There was no mistaking the joy with which Margery Bradburn received their news, and her delighted surprise at their unexpected visit turned to near rapture when Ben explained they were in Middledeane with two purposes in mind, the one to see her, the other to make arrangements for their wedding.

'Oh, Tiffany, Tiffany!' she exclaimed, hugging her niece to her. 'I'm so happy—I knew you would find love some day!'

Never had she imagined that deceiving her aunt could make her feel so conscience-stricken. Waves of guilt washed over her as Margery Bradburn mopped the tears of happiness from her eyes. Tiffany struggled for words, but none came and she was grateful for the supporting arm Ben placed around her shoulders as though telling her not to weaken, it was all for the best. Briefly he held her to him before withdrawing his arm, and then revealed to her that he had a great deal of charm as he got her aunt over her emotional moment.

Mrs Bradburn quickly recovered, and before they could stop her, was talking of making all sorts of arrangements for the wedding, '... and I'll get in touch with Plymton's the caterers, and ...'

'Aunty!' At the risk of seeing the pleasure die in her aunt's face, Tiffany just had to stop her. 'Aunty, I'm sorry, but—but we've—we don't want a big wedding.' Tiffany's voice died on her and she looked at Ben to help her out. He did not let her down.

'We want to be married straight away, Mrs Bradburn,' he smiled down at Tiffany. 'Quite honestly. I can't bear the thought of waiting until all the arrangements are made that a large affair would mean.' Then, his charm in evidence once more, 'If you wouldn't mind our settling for a quiet wedding ...'

Margery Bradburn gave in without a fight, and after smiling at Ben turned to her niece to ask gently, 'Will you be inviting your parents, dear?' The question had to be asked, though she knew better than anyone the trauma Tiffany had been put through as a very sensitive child.

Tiffany didn't have time to think about her answer. 'No,' she stated bluntly. Her aunt knew about her parents and wouldn't be put out by her reply, but she felt Ben looking at her, and couldn't return his look. How could she tell him of the hate and suspicion in her parents' marriage? How could she tell him she couldn't bear that any of it should rub off on to her wedding day?

A tense silence followed her refusal to have her parents to see her married, and against her will she found her eyes drawn to Ben and saw his speculative regard on her flushed face. 'I don't suppose they'd come anyway,' she said lamely.

'I don't think they would either, dear,' Margery Bradburn said gently.

After lunch Tiffany and Ben went to see Mr Farrow, the vicar. He was delighted to see Tiffany and it was arranged he would marry them four weeks the following Tuesday.

'I'd like to call and see Colonel Wainwright since we're so near,' Ben told Tiffany as they left the vicarage. 'Marchberrow's only ten miles away.'

'I can walk back to Aunty's,' Tiffany said, thinking Ben meant to go to Marchberrow on his own.

'What sort of fiancée have I got myself?' Ben asked, putting her into his car. 'You're coming with me.'

Tiffany took to the Colonel straight away. He was a born flatterer with a twinkle in his eye, but he was sincere when he congratulated Ben on his future bride, adding, 'If I was thirty years younger, I'd have given you a run for your money, Ben.'

They didn't stay very long, and on the way back to Middledeane, Ben mentioned that he had invited the Colonel to their wedding while she had been sitting in the car and he had stood chatting for a few minutes longer when they had said goodbye.

'I'm glad you invited him,' she said. 'I liked him.' The thought had passed through her mind that she would like the Colonel to give her away, but she hadn't like to suggest it on so short an acquaintance. 'I ...' she began, then thought better of it and closed her mouth.

'I?' Ben prompted.

'I was just going to say I would have liked to have asked him to give me away, but ...'

'Why didn't you ask him?'

'Well, I don't know him very well,' Tiffany replied. 'He might not like the idea.'

'He'll be delighted,' Ben told her. 'I'll ask him if you like.'

'Would you?' she asked, and at her eager question he pulled into the side of the road, stopped the car and turned to look steadily at her.

'You don't think your father will be offended?'

'It's not a question of offending him,' she said. 'I doubt very much if he or my mother will be all that interested.' Her voice was husky as she choked back threatening tears. Her mother had sent her a card at Christmas, but her father hadn't bothered, and her mother's card she knew had only be n sent because she happened to come across her address in her address book when writing out her Christmas cards—birthdays were always forgotten. 'I know it must sound awful to you,' she went on, keeping her eyes glued to her hands in her lap, 'but as far back as I can remember, life with my parents was one big row. They only stayed together because of me, but a day never went by without them reminding me of it, and I ... I was never more grateful than when they split up and I was able to go and live with Aunt Margery.'

Ben placed a hand under her chin and forced her to look at him. He studied her eyes, seemed to see in their depths something of the sensitive child she must have been. It was still there in the love she had for her aunt—wasn't she marrying him basically to save her aunt from further anxiety about her?

'I know you think me hard,' Tiffany said quickly, unable to hold his straight look, but finding it impossible to pull away, 'but if my parents came to the wedding I know they would only fight, and ... and,' a note of defiance crept into her voice as she pictured how it would be, 'and I want my wedding day to be beautiful.' She stopped abruptly, aghast at what she had said. So wanting Ben not to see her as hard as she must seem, she had said that last bit without thinking. Had she given herself away? For a few agonising seconds she felt the colour riot through her skin, then Ben was saying quietly:

'If not having your parents there to see you married will make your day beautiful, so be it,' and then he was placing an arm loosely across her shoulders and drawing her to him.

Tiffany's eyes grew wide as his head came down, and she felt a flicker of panic as the thought came to her that he was going to kiss her mouth. Whether he read the instant's panic in her eyes, she couldn't tell, but his kiss never landed on her mouth, and instead she felt the lightest of kisses settle on her cheek. Then the arm was taken away from her and he was starting up the car, looking over his shoulder as he watched for incoming traffic before pulling out.

There was no time for her to give any thought to what had happened after that, for they were back at her aunt's house having a hurried bite of tea, then they were back on the road driving towards London, and Tiffany dared not give way to her thoughts in case she said something else without thinking.

'I won't come in,' Ben refused the offer, on seeing her to the door of her flat. 'I'm on duty before dawn cracks tomorrow, and I have a few phone calls I want to make before I turn in.'

Left to herself Tiffany wondered if he would be phoning his father in Switzerland, then as her hand strayed to her cheek, a happy glow started to burn within her. Ben's kiss had meant, she felt sure, that he had understood her not asking her parents to the wedding, had understood and not found her wanting. She thought then she would never again doubt her decision to marry him. She wanted her little share of heaven, brief and without passion as it might be—she loved Ben Maxwell, and she was going to have her half a loaf.

The time raced by before Tiffany's last flight prior to her marriage. First of all she saw Admin. about having time off, and found it unnecessary because Ben had already arranged it for her. Then she had to buy something to be married in, and after much searching found exactly what she was looking for. It was a white dress crocheted in cotton, and lined with white satin, and managed to look delicate, demure and elegant all at the same time. It had a fitted bodice and long sleeves, and with it, in sanctity of the occasion on which it would be worn, went the most exquisite little Juliet cap. More than satisfied with her purchase, Tiffany raced back to her flat thinking she would

never be cleared and packed in time. Ben had given her a
key to his apartment so that she could install her clothes
and anything else she didn't want to part with.

Janet's offer to help was gratefully accepted, and the
two girls set about clearing the flat.

'I won't need this, or that,' said Tiffany, holding up her
electric kettle and pointing to the carpet sweeper.

'I'll find homes for them,' said Janet, who seemed to
know scores of people.

The flat looked bare when Tiffany left to go on duty.
Most of her things were now at Ben's place and her flat
echoed hollowly. Only one more night to be spent here,
that would be when she returned from her flight, when
she would stop off here, pick up her suitcase, and the
large paper carrier with her dress and cap in. One more
night in her own bed, then leave the key with Janet who
was going to get rid of everything else before handing the
key over to Morton's. One more night, then she would be
off to Aunt Margery's to help with the last-minute pre-
parations.

Tiffany chewed her bottom lip thoughtfully. She
couldn't help hoping that living with Ben would turn out
all right. Then she gave herself a mental shake; of course it
would be all right. Why, with both of them working and
unless they happened to be on the same flight, she doubted
she would see him all that often. They would probably
only see each other to say hello and goodbye as they
passed on the stairs—somehow that thought wasn't at all
pleasing.

It had been an exhausting flight, her last one as Miss
Nicholls, and Tiffany wanted nothing more than to go to
her flat, and hope that the depression that had suddenly
come over her and added to her weariness would be gone
when she awoke. But any ideas she had of driving to her

flat and going to bed were soundly knocked on the head by her colleagues.

'We're not letting you go without a celebratory drink,' one of the flight engineers declared, and his call was taken up by several others, who needed little excuse for a party.

Knowing she would look a spoilsport if she didn't do as they asked, Tiffany went with them to the staff club and endured their good-humoured leg-pulling for an hour before, on the pretext of having masses to do, she was able to make her escape.

It had been wishful thinking to hope that a glass of something alcoholic might lift her spirits—it hadn't. Only three more days to her wedding; perhaps she needed this holiday, she thought as she climbed the stairs to her flat.

Exchanging her uniform for her housecoat Tiffany realised Ben would be on holiday too, and wondered if he would be going away somewhere. Then her cheeks burned with colour. Was she supposed to go too? All thoughts of sleep immediately left her. There was no earthly reason why Ben should take her on holiday with him—it wasn't a proper honeymoon, was it? Oh, why hadn't she asked him? But how could she?

Another thought struck her—what if Ben didn't intend going away anywhere? What if he meant the two of them to stay at his place together? For a whole week her mind shouted. How could she bear to stay with Ben in the close confines of his apartment for a whole week? She was definitely getting jittery. Brides were supposed to feel like this, so stop worrying, Tiffany, she adjured herself, it will be all right.

The hands of the clock moved slowly round and when it was nearly midnight, Tiffany felt exactly the same, and it still wasn't all right. Pointless going to bed, she knew she wouldn't sleep. Her nerves were stretched with worrying if she was doing the right thing, and the terrible thought struck her what if she and Ben ended up hating each other? It was then she began to feel decidedly weepy.

When a knock sounded on her door she nearly catapulted from the settee, her nerves were so tautly pitched. Who on earth would be calling at this time of night? She hoped it wasn't any of that mad crowd from the staff club coming to finish off the party at her place. Her hair was out of its usual French pleat, and she tucked a loose end behind her ear and tried to force a smile as she opened the door.

'Ben ...' It was barely whispered, and pure shock, since she hadn't expected to see him until they stood side by side in church, had tears rushing to her eyes.

He looked ready to state the reason for his late visit until he saw the gigantic struggle she was having to get her emotions under control.

'What ... ?' he began instead.

But Tiffany didn't wait to hear any more. It was unthinkable that he should see her in tears. She fled, ran to her bedroom and closed the door between them, and was striving so desperately for control that she didn't hear the bedroom door being quietly opened. Was unaware that Ben was behind her until two hands descended and turned her round to face him. He took one look at her strained face, felt her tremble, and on a gentle note she had never thought to hear from him asked:

'What is it, Tiffany?'

Mutely she looked at him, knowing if she said one word she would be crying all over him. And then he was pulling her against his chest, his arms were coming round her, and it was heaven to feel his hand stroking her hair until she felt calmer.

She tried to pull away then. She started saying, 'Oh, Ben, I've been so ... so ...' but could get no further, and gave herself up to the security of being in his arms. How could she explain her doubts and fears to this confident self-assured man? This man who had decided to marry her, and having received her acceptance in all probability thought no more about it.

At last he seemed to think he had held her long enough, and one arm dropped away from her as he led her into the sitting room, his other arm still about her. 'I can see your nerves are shot,' he said quietly. 'Suppose we sit down and you tell me what it is that's bothering you.'

Strangely, none of her thoughts and worries seemed anywhere near as large now that he was there, but Tiffany found herself telling him something of what she had been feeling.

'All the ifs and buts about our marriage came crowding in—I ... I just couldn't think clearly any more,' she told him.

'You're tired, I expect,' Ben told her, sitting on the settee beside her, his arm still around her. 'Added to which you've got a bad case of pre-marriage nerves. What's wrong with you, Tiffany, is nothing but sheer panic, which isn't surprising since it's weeks since we last saw each other —you've probably forgotten what I look like.' He was way off beam there, she hadn't forgotten a thing about him, though she wasn't about to tell him so. 'It's understandable that your ifs and buts should take on enormous proportions,' he went on calmly. 'And the fact that you're tired hasn't helped any.'

Tiffany was prepared to agree with anything he said, and told him she was feeling very much better.

'Good,' he said, and she could have wished he had kept his arm about her as he said it, but he didn't, and she had a dreadful feeling he was now going to leave. She relaxed as she heard him say, 'Now how about making your fiancé a cup of coffee before he makes a hasty exit?' and on a lighter note, 'You'll be getting talked about, entertaining gentlemen callers at this time of night!'

Tiffany shot into the kitchen. This was a new Ben, even more lovable than the one she had thought she had been getting to know. She still hadn't the nerve to ask him what his holiday plans were, but right at this moment it didn't worry her.

Since the other chairs had already gone, she took the coffee into the sitting room and returned to the settee beside him, a feeling of shyness suddenly swamping her.

'Er—did you have any special reason for coming to see me?' she asked, not that it mattered; it was enough that he was here.

'No—I was just passing and happened to look up and see your light was on. I wondered if there were any last-minute problems, so decided to come up.'

She was glad he had, but couldn't think of anything to say to that, so she lapsed into silence until she saw his glance flick round the room and found her tongue.

'Looks a bit bare now, doesn't it?'

'Not to worry—only one more night. You're going down to Middledeane tomorrow?'

'That's right,' she agreed. 'All packed and ready to go. I just have a few last-minute things to do before I take the key in to Janet.'

'You've got your passport?'

'Passport?'

He nodded. 'I thought we'd spend one night in the flat, then go over to Switzerland. I'd like my father to meet you.'

All Tiffany's gremlins disappeared. It didn't matter that the reason Ben was taking her with him was purely in order to set his father's mind at rest. He was taking her with him, and nothing else mattered. She could do nothing about the smile that beamed his way, it lit her eyes and, had she known it, she looked beautiful. Ben looked away from her and she thought she saw a muscle jerk at the side of his throat, but couldn't stop the words that came tumbling from her lips.

'I didn't think you would be taking me on holiday with you,' she blurted out, which caused Ben to glance her way again.

'I've done some odd things in my day, I admit,' he said, 'but it just hadn't occurred to me to go on my honeymoon without my bride.' He waited to see her crimson, she did, and he gave her that half smile that made her heart turn over. 'Are you all right now?' he asked, standing up.

'I'm fine,' she told him.

'Till Tuesday, then, Tiffany,' he said, then she was alone.

CHAPTER FIVE

TIFFANY'S wedding day dawned shining and cloudless. Margery Bradburn came into her bedroom carrying a breakfast tray which brought a protest from her niece, 'Oh, Aunty, you shouldn't have,' but her aunt's wobbly smiled silenced her and Tiffany put her arms round her and thanked her.

Her aunt Margery was doing very well, Tiffany thought, and hadn't cried once that morning. But when she saw her niece in her bridal white, nothing could stop the tears from coming to her eyes. 'Tiffany, you look beautiful,' she cried, peeping over her shoulder to look at her through the full-length mirror of the wardrobe door. Tiffany turned and hugged her aunt, and the moment was relieved when the front door bell sounded, announcing the arrival of Colonel Wainwright.

A friend of Ben's, Dr Ian Repton, was to be the best man, and Tiffany wondered if Ben's father's wife Frances would be in church. She hadn't been able to bring herself to ask him that question.

Neighbours from the village where Tiffany had spent most of her adolescent years were congregated at the entrance of the small village church, and cries of, 'Good luck,' and, 'Doesn't she look lovely?' followed them as, on the arm of Colonel Wainwright, Tiffany entered through the church door. Then she was unaware of anything save that Ben was there. She knew he was aware she had arrived because she saw the man beside him look at her, then turn to say something to him. But he didn't turn round, and she desperately needed to read reassurance in those grey eyes.

Ben's voice was firm and clear as he spoke his vows, while Tiffany's voice came shakily as she began to make her responses, until she felt the warmth of Ben's hand holding hers, and then she knew that everything was going to be all right. The tremor left her voice, and though still quiet, her voice was now as clear as his had been.

He looked at her as he placed the ring on her marriage finger, and that half smile tugged at the corners of his mouth, his eyes taking in the purity of her in her white dress, her newly shampooed hair shining beneath her Juliet cap. Her answering smile caused his fingers to tighten ever so slightly on the hand he was holding, then relaxed, and the service continued.

Margery Bradburn had arranged for a photographer to be on hand when they came out of church, and Tiffany had a few moments in which to catch her breath as she became fully aware she was now married to this rugged man at her side who was laughing at some quip his friend Ian Repton had made.

And then general introductions were being made, Ben making sure her aunt was not feeling left out, and receiving Mrs Bradburn's kiss of congratulation. The smart female standing beside Colonel Wainwright came over to Tiffany, and Ben was introducing her as Frances. Tiffany thought her to be only a few years younger than Ben, probably about thirty-three or four, then Frances was saying, without any sign of the animosity Tiffany had been looking for, 'I'm so pleased to meet you, Tiffany, and I just know you and Ben are going to be very happy,' then she was kissing Tiffany's cheek.

Everybody seemed to be coming over and saluting her in the same fashion, Tiffany thought, as Ben ribbed Ian Repton for holding on to her for too long, for all Ian's kiss, like the others, had landed on her cheek.

Then Tiffany was alone with Ben in his car and they were driving along to the olde-worlde hotel seven miles away where Ben had hired a private room for a celebration meal.

Tiffany was very quiet as they drove along. Back at the church there had been a lot of banter and her mind was busy with the thought that everyone had kissed her— everyone, except Ben. Not that it mattered to her one way or the other, but for the look of the thing he might have given her a peck on the cheek—Aunt Margery was sure to have noticed.

Ben asking, 'What's the matter?' startled her.

'Nothing,' she replied quietly, finding herself unable to look at him, and suddenly he was turning the car off the main road and driving down a secondary road.

'This isn't the way to ...'

His grim, 'I know it isn't,' cut her short.

Then he was pulling over on to the grass verge, and still unable to look at him, Tiffany knew her short answer had upset him. The car stopped and she knew he had turned to look at her.

'Tiffany.'

Just that and no more. It was said quietly, and she knew he was waiting for her to turn and face him. Knowing she would do neither of them any good by ignoring his unspoken request, she slewed around forcing herself to meet his eyes. They were glinting dangerously, she saw but he wouldn't let her back away from his look.

'I cannot accept that "nothing" is wrong,' he told her grittily, 'and I refuse to have our first row within an hour of our being married—so out with it—what's troubling you?'

She opened her mouth, managed to say, 'I ...' and closed it again. Not for the life of her could she tell this platonic husband of hers the truth—the plain unvarnished truth, that she was put out because he hadn't kissed her. He waited for her to add more, then when she didn't, he showed her what she had quite forgotten—that Ben Maxwell was set in a very different mould from any other man she knew, showed her what she had also forgotten, that he had an uncanny knack of knowing exactly what was in her mind.

'If you're aggrieved because I didn't give you the customary kiss at the church,' he ignored her confirming gasp as his arrow scored a direct hit, 'I'll tell you now why I didn't. It wasn't because I hadn't thought of it, because ...' he paused, looked irritated for a moment, then as though searching for words and growing fed up with the need to break something gently to her, his voice altered, lost some of its harshness, and he said, 'Hell, Tiffany, you have no idea how you look—so beautiful—so young—dammit, so virginal!'

Tiffany blushed, more from the thrill of knowing Ben thought she looked beautiful than anything else. Ben witnessed her blush, then told her, no hardness in his voice at all now:

'What I'm trying to say is this—I know you're a strictly marriage-before-bed girl, and right now you're married to me. We both know ours is a marriage made because of a certain set of circumstances, but in a few hours' time we shall be back at the flat on our own.' Tiffany's heart was hop, skipping and jumping about wildly as she looked back at him and tried to see the point he was making, and then he told her, 'It's natural that you're going to feel apprehensive when you're alone with me tonight, so, much as I wanted to join with the others and salute you after our marriage ceremony, I thought it wiser not to give you any cause for nervous speculation when that time comes—— Do you understand me, Tiffany?'

'I didn't think,' she said huskily. Oh, to have his ability to think three moves ahead! He was right, of course. Apart from the newness of moving into a different flat, sleeping in a strange bed, she knew she would be feeling pangs of disquiet left alone with the virile-looking man when darkness descended and she was alone with him.

And then he was saying, 'I know your aunt isn't here to see—and that's what this is all about, isn't it?' Tiffany felt it better not to answer, contenting herself with being glad Ben had no idea her pique hadn't all been on account of her aunt. 'But since you now know the whys and wherefores, I think we should seal our bargain.'

His arm came over her shoulder, and then Tiffany felt herself being drawn towards him, and his mouth was over hers, not seeking and taking, but pleasure-giving and sur-

prisingly gentle. It was the most beautiful kiss she had
ever received. Instinctively she knew he was holding himself in check, knew this wasn't his usual sort of kiss. Then
his one hand gripped hard on her waist, and he drew back,
the long kiss ended.

Tiffany opened her eyes and thought she saw a kindling
of fire in his look—thought he was on the edge of telling
her something, and thoroughly bemused, would have
agreed then to anything he suggested. But all he said as
he turned to start the engine was, 'I think it's time we went
and joined the others, don't you, Mrs Maxwell.'

Of course the 'others' had arrived when they reached
the hotel. They were all beaming, and Ian Repton put it all
into words for them by saying, 'Now there stands a girl
who's been thoroughly kissed!' Tiffany looked across at
her aunt, saw she was laughing with the rest. Tiffany was
happy.

After a lengthy meal, Ben took Tiffany to her aunt's
house to change. She had a new mustard-coloured wool
suit, and what with all the bridal lingerie her aunt had
insisted on giving her, she really did feel like a bride. As
well as quite a few items of wispy underwear, her aunt
had bought her several frothy nighties and one perfectly
lovely nightdress with matching negligee, a dream of white
nylon, ribbon and lace. Tiffany had gone slightly pink
when she had seen it—dear romantic Aunt Margery! She
had folded the nightdress and negligee back into their
swathes of tissue and placed them in their box; she could
never imagine herself wearing them. The other nightdresses, though, would make a nice change from her usual
pyjamas.

When they arrived back at Ben's flat, he carried her
parcels and suitcases into the bedroom that was to be
hers, and Tiffany following into the room gasped in

amazement. Gone were the dull grey walls, replaced by a Wedgwood effect of blue and white. There were even new satiny blue curtains.

'Ben,' she whispered. 'Was ... Did you have this done for me?'

'I didn't think you liked the grey,' he returned matter-of-factly. 'I'll put some coffee on,' he said, and went through the door.

His thoughtfulness touched her deeply. She wished she could do more for him, and had the opportunity since they had both eaten their fill earlier of preparing a snack meal later on.

Towards eleven o'clock a soft yawn escaped her. It would be heaven to get into bed, she thought; the day's events had taken more out of her than she knew. But she felt slightly uncomfortable about telling Ben she wanted to go to bed, though she thanked him silently for that little talk he'd had with her before they'd gone to the reception—without that she knew she would be a jangling mass of nerves.

'Tired?'

'I am a bit.' Trust him not to have missed that yawn.

'I shan't be turning in just yet, so if you'd like to use the bathroom first ...'

He was smoothing out any tension she felt almost without effort, Tiffany realised, as she showered, donned one of her new nightdresses, and wrapped herself in her old, much washed dressing gown. It was pink and fluffy, and she looked very cuddleworthy as with her face free of make-up, she went through to the sitting room intending to give Ben a quick goodnight before scurrying off to her bedroom.

He rose to his feet as she entered, took in her scrubbed appearance and warm dressing gown. 'You look about sixteen,' he said, and came towards her to cup her face in his hands. 'Thank you for today,' he said sincerely, then his lips made brief contact with her scrubbed cheek. 'Goodnight,' he said.

For ages, it seemed, she lay there, her mind reliving the day, then with a contented sigh she at last turned on to her side and fell into a dreamless sleep.

A hand shaking her shoulder awakened her, bringing her up from a deep sleep. For a moment she had no idea where she was and felt fear shoot through her, not recognising in her sleep-drugged mind that the face bending over her belonged to Ben.

The easy look left his eyes as he saw her frightened expression. The coldness in his voice was biting as he said, 'Take that terrified look off your face, I haven't come to claim my conjugal rights—— It's seven-thirty. We catch a plane in an hour.' The door closed behind him with a decisive snap.

Tiffany came rapidly awake. Quickly she sat up, groaned softly when she saw there was a cup of tea reposing on her bedside table. Oh God, what had she done? She doubted she would ever make him understand that it had been a shock to find a man in pyjamas and dressing gown bending over her, his face not registering through her sleep-befuddled brain.

Ben was back to being the unapproachable airline pilot she had always thought him when she joined him, but refusing to be put off she did all in her power to try and recapture the companionship she had thought was beginning to grow between them yesterday. But after ten minutes of chattering about anything that came into her head and receiving his monosyllabic replies, she found her own temper beginning to rise. If he didn't want to talk, that was O.K. by her!

They were stopping overnight at a hotel in Zürich, Ben

deigned to tell her once they were airborne, and would be completing the remainder of their journey by train the next day. And arriving at their hotel, Tiffany discovered he had booked adjoining rooms. He came into her room with her, looked round as if to satisfy himself that it was comfortable and to her liking, then he disappeared through the communicating door, closing it quietly behind him.

Tiffany glared at the closed door and felt her ire rising again. She was in two minds whether or not to turn the key in the lock of the door separating them, thereby having the last word. Then she censured herself for the thought. Ben would only think she was being childish and he probably thought her fear of him this morning juvenile in the extreme as it was.

She heard a door close, heard firm footsteps moving away down the corridor. He had gone out! How could he? without so much as a word to her. Well, if he thought she was going to stay in her bedroom and wait for his return, he could think again! She would give him a few minutes to get clear and then she too would go out.

Zürich was a clean city. Tiffany liked it. There were many shops in which she could wander, and putting Ben firmly from her mind she began to enjoy herself. What woman could resist going through the dress departments of the big stores, she thought, as she strolled through one store after another. She would like to have bought herself something, but Ben had dropped it on her almost at the last moment that they would be coming to Switzerland, and she didn't have any Swiss currency. So although she did see one eye-catching dress, she reluctantly turned her back on it.

She had no idea how long she had been away, but what did it matter how long she'd been, she thought, as she entered through the doors of the hotel. Ben wouldn't have missed her; in all probability he hadn't returned himself.

Barely had she stepped through her door than Ben strode through from his room. He made no attempt to disguise the ice in his eyes, and expecting trouble, Tiffany lifted her chin a few degrees higher. The ice in his eyes was matched by his voice, she found.

'And just where the hell do you think you've been?'

About to say 'Out' Tiffany took another look at his face, and changed it rapidly to, 'Shopping.'

'It didn't occur to you, I suppose, to think to tell me you were going out?'

'You didn't tell *me you* were going out,' Tiffany fired back, while gasping at the man's arrogance.

'Apart from nipping down to the desk to pick up a train timetable, I haven't been out,' was his instant reply. 'As it is I've been kicking my heels for the best part of three hours wondering where the hell you'd disappeared to.'

She was instantly contrite. How could she have thought him so uncaring as to go out and leave her without a word? 'I'm sorry, Ben.' At least they were now talking—was this a chance to patch things up?

Her hopes were doomed to failure; his voice hadn't thawed when he asked, 'Where is this shopping you couldn't wait to do?'

'I didn't buy anything,' she stated, and goaded by the superior male look in his eye, 'I didn't have time to get any Swiss currency, did I?'

'Neither you did,' he said. She saw his hand go to his wallet and was unprepared for his, 'I changed enough sterling for the two of us—I meant to give it to you before we set off this morning, but it slipped my mind.'

She had a fair idea what made it slip his mind too, but as he went to give her the bundle of notes, she knew nothing would make her take it.

'I haven't enough sterling to settle with you.'

A look of sheer amazement passed over his features. 'Good God, I don't want you to pay it back!' Her expression remained mulish. 'You're my wife, Tiffany,' he said, exasperated, and when she still wouldn't take the money from him, he threw the notes on to her bed, and with a disgusted, 'Women!' he slammed back into his own room.

Tiffany had simmered down by the time it came to start getting ready for dinner that night. She had seen nothing of Ben since he had slammed out of her room earlier. She would have to use a little of his money, she realised, her toothpaste would only take another squeeze and she'd die rather than ask if she could use his.

She was bathed and wearing her robe on top of her underclothes, sitting in front of the dressing table applying eye-shadow to her lids, when the door between the two rooms opened. She knew Ben stood there, but she wouldn't look at him though she felt her hand begin to shake as he surveyed her for a long half minute, not coming any further into the room.

'How long is it going to take you to do that?'

'I'll be ready in ten minutes,' Tiffany answered, not looking at him.

'Hmm—that means twenty. Would you mind if I waited for you in the bar?'

She found no amusement in the thought that already she was driving him to drink. Her, 'Not at all,' was offhand, and at his indrawn breath she just had to look at him, and quickly away again, not liking at all the look that met her. She was sure his look said he would like to take some drastic action with her, and she had no idea what. Shake her? Kiss her? The door snapped shut. She was on her own.

Exactly twenty minutes later Tiffany entered the bar.

She saw Ben at once, he was talking to one of the most attractive blondes she had ever seen and she felt nausea rise up and hit her. Pure jealousy, she realised as she stamped down the feeling. Ben and his companion were easily the best looking couple in the room.

He saw her, and stood up as she went to join him. 'At last, darling,' he said, and while she was still recovering from that 'darling', 'I want you to meet an old friend of mine.'

Trust him to have an old friend who looked like this one! Holly Barrington, it appeared, had grown up with him, and on closer inspection Tiffany saw she looked to be about thirty.

'Isn't it marvellous bumping into you like this!' Holly at least was delighted, and from what Tiffany could see Ben was equally pleased. He invited her to join them for dinner at any rate.

Tiffany tried to infuse some warmth in her tones when speaking to Holly, and thought she just about managed it, though from what she could tell Holly wouldn't have worried anyway. She monopolised the conversation, monopolised Ben, and what with her 'Do you remembers' coming out every five minutes, Tiffany was beginning to feel like an unwanted guest at a feast.

Surely he could shrug that possessive hand off his sleeve if he wanted to. And that, Tiffany thought, summed up the whole miserable business—he obviously didn't want to. Holly was off on another of her, 'Do you remember, Ben,' sagas, and Tiffany thought her stifled yawn had gone undetected.

'Are you tired, darling?' she heard Ben say, and realised he was talking to her.

'I am a little,' she confessed, and quite without thinking, 'It was quite late when I got off to sleep last night.' Scarlet colour flooded every part of her, and she felt she would burn with the heat of it as she realised the implication behind her words; last night had been the first night of her honeymoon.

Too embarrassed to look at Ben, she saw Holly was smiling, then daring to look at him, she saw his half smile had turned into a definite grin.

'You go on up, then, Tiffany,' he said with a glance at his unfinished brandy. 'I won't be long myself.'

Tiffany found herself on her feet with Ben standing beside her. 'G-Goodnight,' she stammered to Holly, and fled.

Reaching her room, Tiffany didn't feel any better about what she had just said, but grew calmer as she prepared for bed and felt the comfort of her old fluffy gown around her. Not the sort of dressing gown one would normally take on honeymoon, but then this wasn't a normal marriage and she couldn't help wondering why, since Ben had needed a wife, he hadn't married Holly. She didn't doubt that Holly would be more than willing to fill that role.

The puzzle swung round and around in her brain of why hadn't he asked Holly to marry him, and she could find no answer until, about to give it up, it came to her; Ben needed a wife in order to allay his father's fears. But since he didn't want to be married once his father was well again and once more reunited with Frances, Ben would want to be free—and Holly was not the type to let go.

A movement in the next room alerted her to the fact that Ben was there, and the depression of her thoughts vanished as a small smile played around her mouth. Ben hadn't stayed with Holly for very long after she had left them. The door opened as she stood there watching it, and there was Ben, none of the harshness in his face now that had been there the last time he had opened that door.

'Not in bed yet?' he enquired mildly. 'I thought since you were so late in dropping off last night you were tired?' The colour stormed to her cheeks. 'Yes, you can blush,' he added, and she could have sworn there was a twinkle in his eye as he said it.

So certain was she that Ben had found the incident amusing that the misery that had been her companion for most of the day dissolved, and the thought came that here was the moment to try and put things right between them.

'Ben,' she said, then quickly because she wanted it said and over with, 'Ben, about this morning.' That was as far as she got, as a hard look came to his eyes, she could almost feel the frost piling up inside him. 'P-Please listen to me, Ben,' she went on as he stood stiffly, his eyes piercing through her. If she said this all wrong she would be spending another miserable day tomorrow and she didn't think she could bear that. 'When you woke me this m-morning I was still half asleep——' she looked away from him, aware she was gabbling now. 'I ... I've never been woken by a man before and your face didn't register. I was in a strange bed, a strange room, and ... and there was this man bending over me—— D-don't you see, Ben—I didn't know it was you.' She came to the end, suddenly convinced she had just made a complete and utter fool of herself, convinced that it didn't matter to him what she had felt at the time.

Then he was leaving his position by the door, coming to place his hands lightly on her shoulders, and she realised she hadn't made a fool of herself after all, for he was saying, 'Thank you for explaining all this to me, Tiffany. I confess, seeing the terror in your eyes this morning threw me. I thought we'd got on quite well last night, thought I had your trust. Your cringing away from me this morning as though I was some lustful animal with rape in mind sickened me.' Tiffany looked up at him then, as it dawned on her that Ben had a sensitivity she hadn't associated with him. 'Since we're being so honest with each other,' he said, giving her a smile that played havoc with her, 'I'll confess it was touch and go whether I came back and gave you something to be terrified about.'

Tiffany's face burned furiously as the import of what he had just said hit her. 'You wouldn't have?'

'Wouldn't I?' She couldn't doubt it. 'Who would have stopped me?'

She knew her strength would have been puny against his, and paled at the thought of what could nearly have happened. She loved this man she had married, wanted with all her heart to be a wife to him, but to be taken in anger, she felt then, would have finished their short marriage before it got started.

'Don't worry about it,' he said quietly, his hands leaving her shoulders as he turned to go. 'It didn't happen, did it?'

Tiffany was glad she'd had the courage to tell him what she had, for after that the tension eased between them. Ben was certainly his most amiable as he came into her room the next morning and escorted her down to breakfast. They left Zürich without seeing Holly Barrington again, and arriving in Davos they went by taxi to their hotel, where Tiffany found he had booked a suite of rooms for their stay, comprising of two bedrooms, a sitting room and a bathroom. He told her to pick which bedroom she wanted and they both went to unpack. Her unpacking didn't take long, but she took the chance to change from her travel clothes into a green trouser suit before she joined Ben in the sitting room. She saw his eyes flick over her, hoped he thought she was looking as good as her mirrored reflection had told her she was, but knew better than to expect him to say so.

'I thought we'd visit my father this afternoon,' he told her. 'I spoke with him on the phone yesterday and he's looking forward to meeting you.'

Not sure what to expect, Tiffany set out with Ben later that afternoon and found it an exhilarating fifteen-minute walk to the hospital. But when they got there, she discovered it was nothing at all like a hospital. It was a big house set in a mountainside full of pine trees, and on stepping inside, instead of the clinical atmosphere she had anticipated with probably a nurse or two scurrying about, she saw it was homely and the girl who approached them and directed them to a lounge was not a nurse at all but a maid. She spoke a kind of Swiss German which Ben understood more easily than Tiffany, and told them Mr Maxwell would join them shortly.

'Isn't your father in bed?' Tiffany asked Ben when the maid had gone, trying not to let the nervousness she was feeling at this meeting show.

'He was at first,' Ben told her, and if he too was feeling nervous, for if Harvey Maxwell didn't believe his son was in love with the girl he had married two days ago, then it would all have been in vain, he hid it well. 'He has not been a bed patient for some time now, though he still has periods of enforced bed rest—but the air here is so pure, just the simple act of breathing is clearing his trouble.' He broke off, obviously listening.

Tiffany heard it too, the sound of movement outside in the hall, and her eyes flew to Ben as she realised that when the door opened, they would be face to face with his father.

Ben's arm reached out for her, and without a second's thought she went to him, felt his arm close her to him, and felt comfort from that contact. When Harvey Maxwell opened the door, it was to see his son and new daughter-in-law standing together, his son holding his bride close to him. There was a silence that seemed to stretch endlessly as Harvey Maxwell looked from one to the other, though in reality Tiffany realised it only lasted about two seconds, then Ben was taking her with him over to his father, his arm dropping away from her as the two men greeted each other, Ben saying, 'Hello, Dad,' and she could have sworn his voice had thickened slightly as, his greeting over, he turned to include her and said, 'I want you to meet Tiffany.'

Tiffany wanted to speak, but couldn't find her voice. Wanted to stretch her hand out and say, 'Believe me, you have nothing to worry about. Ben doesn't love Frances in the way you think he does', but she couldn't say anything, do anything except just look at the man who was tall like his son, severe-looking like him, and so very like Ben apart from his more lined face and white hair in contrast to Ben's almost black hair. In turn, she was aware that Harvey Maxwell was studying her, realised he didn't want her to say anything. And then, their eyes fixed on each other, Tiffany saw the most beautiful smile she had ever seen on a man light up Harvey Maxwell's face.

'So you're the one who finally anchored him down, eh?' he said.

And then Tiffany's voice escaped from its bonds of fear. 'It took some doing,' she acknowledged, 'but yes—I managed it,' and because she knew he had accepted what Ben wanted him to believe, a beaming smile of her own broke from her, and she felt herself being hauled into a hug that was purely and simply a mixture of heartfelt relief and happiness on the part of Harvey Maxwell.

They didn't stay longer than an hour. Ben, more attuned than Tiffany for signs of tiredness in his father, said they would leave him so he could rest and would call and see him the next day.

Sensing that Ben was occupied with his own thoughts, Tiffany was silent as they walked back, and the hotel was within sight before Ben came out of his reverie.

'So you managed to anchor me down, did you?'

Tiffany looked back at him quickly, wondering if her agreeing with his father had offended him for all she couldn't see that she could have done anything else. And then she saw that Ben was grinning down at her, a grin that was so infectious she could do no other than grin straight back.

'The bigger they are the harder they fall,' she said brightly, and although that meant nothing, for they both knew there was not the remotest chance he would fall for her, she was happy, though she had to look away from him in case his grin changed to a frown.

Once the silence between them had been broken, Tiffany found a flood of questions she wanted to ask him. 'How do you think your father is looking?'

'About the same as last time I saw him, I think,' he told her, and sent her spirits sky high adding, 'Seeing you has lifted him.'

'Do you think so?'

'Sure of it,' he confirmed. 'You couldn't see his face when he was hugging you—— At a guess I'd say you're the best medicine he's had in a long time.'

Her spirits soared even higher. She knew it hadn't been her personally that had been the tonic Harvey Maxwell needed, but her as Ben's wife. It made her feel her marriage, as Ben had said, wasn't all one-sided, if seeing her had lifted his father.

As she lay in bed that night, Tiffany reflected that it had been a good day. Not once had that harsh look she hated shadowed Ben's face. And after an early dinner they had spent over an hour or so walking round Davos, not too large a place, but a picturesque spot. Then back at their hotel after saying she didn't want a drink and that she thought she would turn in, tired but relaxed, she had left him to his nightcap.

She had heard him moving about in his room. He must have seen her light on, she reasoned, for quietly he had opened her door, seen her ensconced beneath the covers and awake, and while her heart had hurried up its beat he had said, 'Thought you might have dropped off and forgotten to put your light out.' As an afterthought he'd asked, 'Any problems?' She had shaken her head, knowing her voice would come out all husky if she tried to speak, and he had left her with a quiet, 'Goodnight.'

She lay sleepless for some time after that, while her heart settled down to its normal beat, basking in the warm glow, the protected feeling his 'Goodnight' had given her. Her warm glow disappeared as the startling thought came to her that she would hate it if his feelings for her were fatherly. What feelings? Ben felt nothing for her, fatherly or otherwise.

It was three o'clock before she finally dropped off to sleep, consequently she was in no mood for Ben coming into her room and disturbing her sleep.

'Come on, show a leg,' he wakened her. 'I want to take you up Schatzalp this morning.'

Need he be so energetic? Just five more minutes, that was all she wanted. 'Go away,' she said, burying her head from the rude sunlight that streamed through the opened curtains.

Suddenly she was cold. Cold and indignant, as he did no more than fling the bed covers away from her semi-sleeping form. Instantly Tiffany came wide awake, scarlet colour adding to the pink cheeks of sleep as she became aware that he was standing looking down at where her nightdress, pretty and feminine as it might be, had ridden up during the night and was now revealing almost the full length of her naked shapely thigh. The covers were replaced before she could make a grab at them, but that didn't make her feel any better.

'Hell, Tiffany, I'm sorry,' he was the first to recover as she turned her head away speechless. 'Don't be upset, sweetheart.' His voice, concerned and kind did nothing to mollify her. Then, exasperated, his voice came again. 'Hell's bells, how was I to know—I'd put you down as being strictly the pyjamas type.'

Her, 'Thank you very much,' was pure acid, and she didn't take kindly to the laugh he did nothing to smother either.

'I am your husband after all,' he said easily. 'If I can't look at—er—your delights, who can?' Tiffany was not to be plagued out of her ill humour, and heard Ben give a resigned sigh before he said, 'Well, are you going to get yourself up—or do you want me to do it for you?'

Her, 'No, I'm not,' was changed rapidly to a, 'Yes, I will.' Then she opened her stubbornly tightly closed eyes, and said clearly and loudly, 'Will you get out!' It didn't help matters to hear his laugh as he obeyed her instructions, for all she couldn't help thinking it a lovely sound.

Once bathed and dressed she felt half ashamed of her bad temper—It still rankled with her that he thought her 'strictly the pyjamas type'; she had Aunt Margery to thank that she wasn't any longer. But not being one to bear a grudge, despite the fact she had exchanged barely a civil word with him as they sat down to breakfast, before she had started on her second cup of coffee Tiffany knew she couldn't keep up her unfriendly attitude for much longer.

And so after suffering one of Ben's long intent looks, she knew she would have to do something about it.

'I'm sorry I was such a grouch this morning,' she said quietly while she had the courage, adding lamely, 'I didn't sleep very well last night.'

'Any special reason for that?' She should have known he was too quick for her.

'Strange bed, I expect.' Not much of a reason, she knew, particularly as in their line of work they spent very little time in their own beds in their own homes, but Ben didn't press her further, and anyway her aim had been achieved, the ice that had been forming between them was broken.

Climbing up the twisting pathway of Schatzalp, for Ben scorned the use of the cable car, Tiffany felt completely at one with him, particularly since after she stumbled at one point he did no more than tuck her hand into the crook of his arm saying, 'Here, hang on to me.' Tiffany left her hand there until they reached a part on the mountain that housed a restaurant.

They stood together surveying the valley below. She could clearly see a church spire nestling between a cluster of buildings. She thought she would never forget the picture of the snow-topped mountain opposite, the giant fir trees taking on a silhouette of silver as the sunlight tiptoed through their branches. She was loath to move, for Ben seemed as content as she; she thought he shared the same magic of this moment and she wanted to hold on to it for as long as she could. She felt him take her hand as a gossamer thread of enchantment stole around her, but was afraid to look at him in case he wasn't feeling the magic too. Then his grip on her hand tightened and she just had to look at him. Then as a smile of pure happiness started to tug for release because his own expression was gentle,

the gossamer thread was snapped as a voice she had heard
before hailed them.

'Ben—I knew you'd be here!'

Tiffany, who had never hated anyone in her life, felt at
that moment, as Ben let go her hand, she could cheerfully
have pitched Holly Barrington down the mountainside.

CHAPTER SIX

THE remainder of their holiday—the word honeymoon
was a misnomer—was spent with Holly making up an
uneven trio wherever they went. Not that Tiffany ever
heard Ben actually ask her to join them, but somehow she
was always there. In the end Tiffany tried to accept her,
and the more she got to know her, she was surprised to
find given different circumstances, she could well have
liked her. She received an impression that somehow or
other Holly's high spirits were covering up some hurt, and
being softhearted, as their holiday drew to a close it was
she who would say to Ben, 'Shall I ask Holly to join us?'
And if he thought she was pleased to have Holly with
them, so much the better, for after that moment before
Holly had joined them on Schatzalp when she felt sure
she had been ready to tell Ben she loved him, Tiffany was
now on guard that such a moment should never come
again. They had visited his father for the last time yesterday
and were catching an early train for Zürich, then taking
off for London in the late afternoon.

It was with mixed feelings that Tiffany left their hotel
suite. Ben had reverted to being the taciturn man she had

first known, and try as she might she could not put her finger on what had gone wrong between them as she acknowledged then that she had been secretly hoping that this week might cement a foundation for a marriage that need not be ended. She sighed, realising the forlornness of that hope. Why, it had been only last night that he had snapped at her as if he didn't even like her very much. She had awakened in the night, and for some unknown reason she just had to know what time it was, but when reaching for her watch remembered she had left it in the bathroom. So donning her fluffy dressing gown she had opened her bedroom door and had been shaken, believing Ben to have been in bed hours ago, to find him still up.

'My watch,' she had said by way of explanation, feeling disconcerted that he had moved from his chair to come to where she was standing as if suspecting she might be ill or something. 'I . . . I left it in the bathroom,' she added, and made to walk past him, only because she was beset by nerves or maybe she wasn't fully awake, she had stumbled against him, and for one heavenly moment felt his arms around her as they had come automatically to steady her. She cursed herself for her weakness that instead of moving away from him, she had melted against him, only to hear the rasp of his voice as hard as flint saying:

'Can't you look where you're going?'

Never again would she melt against him, she vowed as coming fully awake she'd snapped back, 'Sorry, sir,' for all the world as though they were on duty and she was playing stewardess to his grumpy captain.

Nothing had changed when they reached his apartment —nothing, she thought dully, except a worsening in their relationship. Oh well, she thought, with a resigned shrug, he would be on duty tomorrow and she herself the day after, perhaps when they met again they both would be in happier frames of mind.

Midway through her unpacking Tiffany paused. Her mind had been eaten up most of the day with what a bear Ben was, but was it all his fault? He hadn't asked her to get all twisted up inside over him, and if she was brutally honest—far from making herself lovable this week, in order that he shouldn't find out how she felt about him, she had at times, she realised, been downright unlovable. She knew then that if the rest of the time spent together before their marriage ended was not to be spent in constant snapping and ill humour, she would have to make some effort to be the girl she had been before she had fallen in love with him.

With her new resolution upon her, she went in search of him, her stomach fluttery, having no idea quite what she was going to say to him. She saw the back of him through his open bedroom door. He must have heard her, for he turned as she stood on the threshold of his room. Seeing his face unsmiling, his eyes cold, Tiffany's good intentions abruptly left her, though she had to have some excuse for standing there.

'W-would it be all right if I made a c-cup of tea?'

'Good God, girl,' he barked at her. 'You live here, don't you?'

Hurriedly she turned away, but quick as she was, was not fast enough to hide the hurt his tone caused.

'Tiffany.'

She hesitated, and felt his hand on her arm turning her to face him, her eyes large and misty with controlled tears as she faced him.

'I'm sorry I hurt you,' he said quietly. 'I'm afraid I overlooked the fact that you don't yet feel at home. It is your home, though, Tiffany—and I want you to be happy here.'

When he spoke like that she could forgive him anything. His apology gave her the strength to ask, 'Can't we be friends, Ben?'

'We have been a bit left-footed, haven't we?' he agreed, and as that smile she loved so much broke from him, she beamed back, eager for the chance of a fresh beginning. Only half aware of what she was doing, she reached up and kissed his cheek. Then, aghast at what she had done, she made to turn, only to find he still had his hand on her arm.

'It's almost worth having a spat with you, Tiffany—you make up so delightfully.'

The teasing note in his voice stayed with her as she beat a hasty retreat into the kitchen. And it was just like being married when he joined her a few minutes later asking, 'Have you made that tea yet?'

Within an hour of being back at work Tiffany was in full swing, and within two hours it was as though she had never been away at all as she coped with the rush and bustle of getting airborne. After Ben had gone yesterday she had raced round making the apartment immaculate for his return, and since they had already had one spat over money and she daren't offer him the rent money she had paid Mr West, she had hared round the supermarket and had left his cupboards and icebox bulging.

Throughout the flight her thoughts would turn again and again to him. This flight would take three weeks, she just hoped his off-duty would coincide with hers.

At their various stop-overs she had spent some time on her own, some time going about with the crowd, and when on the return journey they stopped over in Singapore and Michael Croft, the co-pilot, asked her to join him for dinner, she assumed there would be a few other stewardesses and crew present, and accepted. But when she joined him later after changing out of her uniform, she saw Michael was alone.

'Where is everybody?' she asked.

'They've gone off somewhere,' he told her, and as she looked at him, only then did it dawn on her that Michael's invitation had not included anyone else.

She blamed herself for not thinking to ask when he had issued his invitation, but short of telling him she wasn't hungry, when in truth she was starving, there was little she could do about it, and since they both had to eat ...

'Where to, Michael?' she asked.

Michael was good company and over their meal they chatted mainly about the Airline—it was common ground since they both worked for the same company. Tiffany enjoyed her meal but was looking forward to returning to her hotel and getting into bed, reflecting that one had to be as fit as a racehorse to keep up with the pressures of the job, when suddenly, out of the blue, Michael asked:

'What happened to Nick Cowley?' Tiffany looked at him, didn't like at all the accusing note in his voice, but before she could say anything he was saying to her utter astonishmen, 'I suppose he wasn't good enough for you either.'

'What on earth do you mean?'

'Come off it, Tiffany,' Michael said aggressively. 'You know damn well what I mean. One minute you were all lovey-dovey with Nick, then as soon as you found out Ben Maxwell was loaded you couldn't drop Nick fast enough.'

To say 'What do you mean?' again would have been farcical, but she only just bit the words back. She had never known Michael so belligerent; he was certainly wound up over something, and what was he saying about Ben being loaded? It was news to her ...

'You were my girl,' Michael went on nastily, 'and

played me for a sucker, didn't you?' Open-mouthed Tiffany stared at him. 'You couldn't wait to latch on to Nick, then before the poor devil knew what had hit him, it was bye-bye, Nick, wasn't it?'

'Michael, for goodness' sake!' If it hadn't been for the company rule that flight deck members were not to consume alcohol twenty-four hours before a flight, she would have said he had been drinking.

'It's true, isn't it?' he persisted.

'I don't know what you're talking about,' Tiffany said sharply, her temper beginning to rise.

'I'll spell it out for you, then, Tiffany *dear*,' he said sneeringly. 'First you try me out and when I think everything's coming up roses, you throw me over for Nick Cowley, who just happens to have a bigger bank balance than me, and when Nick thinks he's on cloud nine, what happens, along comes Ben Maxwell who could buy Nick's father out any time he wanted to, and hey presto, it's goodbye Nick time.'

Tiffany had heard enough; to stay and tell Michael he couldn't be more wrong was not in her mind at all. She got up and left him right there, hurrying outside, grateful to be away from him—he must be mad! Just what had he been saying? That she was a gold-digger? That Ben had money?

She was almost at her hotel before her temper had cooled sufficiently for her to begin to see Michael more objectively. Had she thrown him over? Of course she hadn't. He had never been her regular boy-friend, for one thing. Everyone at Coronet, everyone who flew, that was, knew that a flying career meant a disrupted social life. There had been times when she hadn't seen Michael Croft for weeks on end, so how could he have thought they were going steady? She was sure she had never given him to understand that she was 'his girl'. And as for throwing Nick over for Ben—if Michael only knew the half of it!

Fed up suddenly, Tiffany thought of her new home. She would be glad to get back. Life came to her and her eyes shone at the thought of maybe seeing Ben, even if only for a few hours. Her cheeks flushed at the thought, she entered her hotel and went to the desk for her key. So deeply were her thoughts with Ben she didn't notice Sheila Roberts coming to collect her key at the same time.

'You're back early.' Tiffany turned at the sound of Sheila's voice. 'I thought I saw you going out with Michael Croft.'

'Hello, Sheila—yes, you did.'

'Up to his old tricks again, was he?'

'Old tricks?' Tiffany repeated in surprise.

'Surely you're not going to tell me he didn't make a pass at you?'

Really, at times Sheila Roberts was just too much! Whatever Tiffany answered to that remark would be embroidered upon and related to the rest of the crowd. 'I wouldn't dream of telling you anything, Sheila,' Tiffany said with more calm than she felt. 'Goodnight.'

Perhaps she was just weary after nearly three weeks of flying she thought as she waited for sleep to take her that night, but the flat she shared with Ben was very appealing just then. She toyed with the idea of ringing the apartment to see if he was home. What wouldn't she give to hear his voice, matter-of-fact, calm, and speaking from home. Sleep was very far away; she knew it was going to be a long night, and it was.

Michael Croft kept out of her way on the home flight, for which she was well pleased. She felt she had nothing to say to him, and since he so obviously bore her a grudge, he was best left alone.

It was with a feeling of lightheartedness that she assisted the last passenger off the plane before going to join the other stewardesses with checking the bar and attending to the paper work involved. When at last she was free to go she made for the car park. Would Ben be home? She hoped so. She could have gone to the Crewing Office and found out if he was flying, but she doubted her ability to hide her emotions if she was told he was away.

Disappointment hit her when she saw his car wasn't outside the building, and calling herself all sorts of an idiot for feeling this way, she took her key from her bag and let herself into the apartment. In the act of placing her suitcase down on the floor and turning to secure the door behind her, she heard a small sound and froze before turning to spin round.

How she checked the beaming smile that winged from her heart she didn't know, but it had been a near thing as she saw Ben standing in the kitchen doorway, a lock of hair falling across his forehead. Just how did one greet a platonic husband—even if you were in love with him? What would he do, for instance, if she obeyed her first instinct and flung her arms around him? She couldn't, wouldn't shake hands with him, that would be too much; all these thoughts flashed through her mind before Ben took the indecision from her.

'You must have smelled the tea-pot,' he said easily. 'Have a good trip?'

'Not bad,' she answered. She had hardly been able to wait to get back and to be greeted by 'You must have smelled the tea-pot' was something of a let down, but then what had she expected?

She followed him into the kitchen telling him about her trip. She was in two minds about telling him about Michael Croft, then realised that he couldn't possibly be interested.

She wanted to ask him how long he would be home, even had the words formed to ask, 'When are you on duty again?' 'When—er—when d-did you get home?' she asked, and because that wasn't what she had meant to ask at all, her cheeks went pink, and not waiting for his answer she collected her case and went to her bedroom.

Idiot! Idiot! Why couldn't she have waited for his answer? At the very least he would think her downright rude in asking a question and not waiting around to hear his reply.

A movement at the door had her startled eyes going to it to see Ben there, his eyes going to the case she had started to unpack. 'Brought your tea in,' he said going over and placing it on her bedside table and then coming back to look at her. 'Incidentally, I got in a couple of days ago.' Her colour surged anew and she dared a glance at him, expecting sarcasm to follow. But his look, though cool, surprised her in that it was not unfriendly. 'Feeling a bit uptight?' he asked. 'Don't fight it, Tiffany—it's natural,' and as she seemed incapable of saying anything at that moment with Ben talking reassuringly to her, he went on, 'It's almost a month since we last clapped eyes on each other, and as ours isn't a very usual—arrangement, it's not surprising that you should feel that way.' His half smile came, and with it she thought she saw a hint of devilment there, and it came to her that not only had he discerned how she was feeling, he also knew she wasn't going to carry on unpacking while he stood there to witness her bits-of-nonsense underwear being brought out on display.

'On second thoughts,' he said, 'bring your tea into the sitting room—come and talk to me.'

Feeling slightly foolish, even though Ben had done all he could to put her at her ease—if you discounted that devilish look towards her suitcase, she thought—Tiffany followed him, tea in hand, into the sitting room.

'Thank you for making the place so nice for me to come home to,' he said, as they sat down. 'I've been in the habit of having a blitz once a month, but I appreciate your woman's touch about the place.'

She had forgotten the polishing and cleaning she had done before leaving, but the arrangement of grasses and beech leaves on a table to the right of the window were there to remind her.

'It was a pleasure,' she said quietly.

'Was it?'

He was looking at her intently. What was he looking for? she wondered. Was she giving too much away? Whether she was or not, she found it impossible to lie to him.

'It was,' she confirmed, and had a sudden dreadful thought that perhaps she had taken too much on her behalf, for all he had thanked her for doing it. 'Y-You don't mind my clearing up a bit?'

His expression hardened. 'I don't want to have to tell you again, Tiffany,' he said shortly. 'This is your home.'

Turning her face from him, Tiffany finished her tea. Ben had been trying to make her feel at ease, and she had spoilt it. He had now turned cold towards her, and it was obvious there was nothing more to say. 'I'll go and unpack,' she said, rising from her chair. She couldn't get to her room fast enough.

She stayed there for a long time. She would have stayed there longer had it not occurred to her suddenly that with Ben being so touchy about her regarding the apartment as her home, it wouldn't surprise her if he didn't come in any minute and tell her to make herself at home in the sitting room. Without stopping to think further she went to leave her room and opened the door to see him just about to open it, and it became clear he was set on doing all he could to make her feel as though she belonged.

'I was just coming to ask what you're going to cook for my supper.'

'You're not going out?' His face hardened at her words, and Tiffany stifled a sigh—she'd been trying so hard not to let him see how pleasing his words had sounded in her ears, she had spoken off the top of her head.

'Are you?' he shot at her.

'N-no.' Oh, what was the use? As he had said, she was uptight, so uptight she couldn't be natural with him. After so looking forward to being with him, spending as much time as she could in getting to know him, she was ruining everything. 'Ben—Ben, I'm sorry,' she apologised, hoping he wouldn't ask what she was saying sorry for. 'L-like you said, I'm uptight.'

With relief she saw his face relax slightly and she went with him into the sitting room. 'What you need is a drink. Sit down, I'll fix one for you.'

The drink certainly helped to steady her nerves and she was much more as ease as she followed him into the kitchen some time later. Ben had said he would cook the supper after all until she had told him she wanted to do it, and after a steady look at her, he had given way

'By the way,' he said, opening one of the bulging cupboards, 'thanks for getting the shopping in. How much do I owe you?'

'Ben!' Tiffany was affronted. 'Please don't make me accept payment—I enjoyed doing it.'

He gave her a level look, and she knew he wasn't pleased. 'All right,' he conceded at last. 'I'll let you get away with it this time. But if you're going to keep the larder stocked, I insist on giving you a housekeeping allowance.'

'I couldn't possibly take it!' Her refusal was quick and

instinctive, and seeing his set face, she added more slowly, 'Please try to understand, Ben, it's the least I can do.' Oh God, his brow was coming down in a dark frown, any minute now he would be calling her 'Nicholls'. He was so darned proud, she thought, forgetting for the moment that she too had pride in full measure. 'Look at it from my point of view,' she carried on, wondering how she had the nerve in the face of his stiff, grim-faced opposition. 'I'm not paying rent now, I'm earning good money, and ... well, I ...' she took a deep breath as his lips tightened still further, and plunged on, 'Well, I feel I should pull my weight.'

'Don't be so damned ridiculous,' he said, ice in every word. 'I don't want your money,' and as if that settled the whole argument, he added snappishly, 'You're my wife,' and left her.

She would love to have banged the kitchen door after him as anger she hadn't known she was capable of feeling overwhelmed her, and she stood glaring at the open doorway. Autocratic swine! She knew he wouldn't be the first to climb down—well, it wouldn't be her this time. Last time it had been she who apologised, and she wasn't going to go through the rest of their marriage saying she was sorry. 'You're my wife', he had said, and just what did that mean? Obviously in his view that while she was married to him his pride would not allow her to contribute to any of the household expenses.

Knowing she couldn't stand glaring at the space where his arrogant back had disappeared through until it was time to go to bed, she found some steak in the fridge and began to prepare their meal, and had a lovely time giving vent to her feelings by banging the juices with a wooden meat mallet. She felt much better afterwards, though she couldn't help looking a little shamefaced when she looked up and saw Ben watching her from the doorway for all the world as if he knew she had imagined she was knocking some reason into his stubborn head.

He came to where she stood, taking the meat hammer from her and placing it on the worktop. Then putting his hands on her shoulders he turned her round to face him.

'I stand by what I said, Tiffany,' he told her seriously, 'but since I'm back on duty tomorrow morning, do you think we can call a truce for this evening?' Tiffany looked at him, mutiny in every line, and then her heart began to thud as he pulled her closer to him. She felt his warm lips briefly on hers and closed her eyes as the ice in her melted, and came back to earth, opening her eyes quickly as he put her away from him saying, 'You're not the only one who can make up nicely, you know.' And as her voice refused to make any answer, being stuck somewhere in her throat, he added, 'Anyway, you were looking a mite dangerous with that meat basher in your hands.' And suddenly they were both laughing.

Later that evening Tiffany rang her aunt and as soon as Mrs Bradburn heard Ben was working the next day, she invited Tiffany down to Middledeane. 'You'll be feeling lonely when Ben has gone,' she urged.

Tiffany knew her aunt was right, but if she stayed in the flat she felt he would seem nearer somehow, and she searched in her mind for a reason to give her for not going without Ben being aware of the real reason, for he was in the same room and although he was buried behind a newspaper, there was no guarantee he wasn't hearing what she was saying.

'I have a few things I really must attend to, Aunty. Do you mind if I leave it until next time?'

'All right, dear. Perhaps you both could come if Ben is

free at the same time? I'd love to have you both to stay with me.'

Ben put down his paper when Tiffany's call had ended, enquiring, 'Is your aunt well?'

Unsure now what she had replied to her aunt's invitation that they both visit her in Middledeane, but thinking he would think it odd if she didn't mention it and he had guessed from what had been said anyway, she told him, and stared at him in amazement when he said:

'I should like that—we'll try and fix something up.'

Masking her surprise, Tiffany felt happiness flood through her. To think she had always thought him to be standoffish and arrogant! True, there were still times when that arrogance showed through, but she was getting to know a different Ben, a warmer man than she had thought him to be, and not only did she love him, but she was beginning to like him as well.

After that the evening passed without strain, and when Ben got up and went into his bedroom for something, Tiffany got up to make some coffee, reflecting that after such a terrible beginning when she had let herself into the flat, the evening was exceeding her expectations, for not one cross word had escaped either of them since Ben had kissed her and made up.

He was back in the sitting room when she returned with the tray of coffee and he came to take it from her and set it down on a small table nearby. Then straightening up he stood in front of her, effectively blocking her way if she didn't want to squeeze by him or take the long route round the back of the settee, which would not only seem silly, but look ridiculous. So she stood where she was and looked at him with a question in her eyes.

'I forgot to give you your engagement ring,' he said

casually, and putting his hand into his trouser pocket, pulled out a small square box and handed it to her.

'My wh-what?' her astonishment was apparent as she gazed at him.

'Don't you think you'd better look and see if you like it?' Wordlessly Tiffany tore her eyes away from him, her brain numb as she gazed at the box he had given her. 'I thought you would prefer something plain, but I can change it if you'd prefer something fussy.'

She was overcome as she opened the box to see he had bought her a beautiful solitaire diamond. 'It's lovely!' escaped her, and then as the thought raced in that he had gone to the trouble to select it for her, even though common sense followed and said it was probably only because his father and her aunt would expect to see an engagement ring complementing the wedding band she wore, her voice became decidedly wobbly, and she was too stunned to say more than, 'Oh, Ben ...'

'Don't cry all over it or it'll melt!'

She looked mistily at him, blinking back the tears that threatened. 'You didn't have to,' she said huskily.

'Do you like it?' he ignored her protest.

'It's beautiful,' she told him, 'but much too expensive,' and much as she would love to have worn it even for a short while, she made to give it back to him. 'I can't take it, Ben,' she said quietly. 'I can't let you spend your money on me like this,' then hurriedly as he looked ready to explode, 'I would be giving it back to you when our marriage is over anyway.' The earlier atmosphere of calm hadn't lasted very long, she thought, as she waited for his volcanic eruption.

There was no doubting his coldly controlled anger, as he said, 'The ring is yours, Tiffany, to keep, regardless of whether or not we part—— Is that clear?'

His quiet anger was unarguable with and though words sprang to her lips Tiffany took one look at the granite hardness in his face and thought better of it. The mood he was in now, he looked capable of anything.

The coffee was drunk in grim silence, Tiffany having the greatest difficulty in swallowing hers, though not prepared to let him see he had defeated her by going to bed without any. Her coffee cup empty, honour satisfied, she stood up, and forced herself to wish him a cool. 'Goodnight.'

His, 'Goodnight,' was chilling. She made it to her bedroom thinking she'd give anything to be able to have a good cry, but she felt beyond tears. Again she recalled the eagerness with which she had hurried to the flat, her every hope pinned on Ben being there, and she could have broken her heart, she felt so utterly despairing. 'Regardless of whether or not we part,' he had said, almost as if there was some doubt about it. She took no joy from that statement, the look that accompanied his words had told her the sooner it ended the better he would like it.

About to get undressed, she became aware she was clutching the box containing the ring. Without conscious thought the box was opened. It really was beautiful and as though in a trance Tiffany slipped the solitaire next to her wedding ring, knowing it would fit as Ben already had her ring size.

She stood looking at it for some time, then suddenly lifted her head, her admiration of the ring forgotten. Ben was outside her door, she heard his quiet, 'Tiffany,' but remained motionless for several seconds until she heard him move away. She had no idea what he wanted, but knew she would not be able to cope with his temper, might even add a little of her own. But the cold anger that had bit into her when she had wanted to return his ring was something outside her experience and she couldn't face it again, not tonight anyway.

Almost furtively in case he should hear and know she was not already in bed, Tiffany eased a drawer open and took out one of her new nightdresses. Aunt Margery had done her proud with her trousseau, she thought, not for the first time. She shook out the nightie that was a dream of lemon nylon and lace and popped it over her head; it concealed her figure but was fine enough to torment the imagination of any new husband. Oh, Aunty, Tiffany groaned inwardly, if only you knew ... ! Getting into bed, she willed sleep to come and take her into oblivion; the engagement ring still on her finger was small comfort to her tortured thoughts. Ben was going off early in the morning and it could be months before she saw him again.

A nagging pain in her jaw brought Tiffany up from the depths of sleep. She tried pressing her cheek into the pillow, but the pain was still there, and after a few minutes of wrestling against toothache and the need for sleep, her toothache won and she sat up, switching on her bedside lamp and reaching for her watch. A quarter to one. She looked about her helplessly, not wanting to make a noise, but knowing with the ache in her jaw going from pain to agony she couldn't put up with it for much longer without trying to do something about it.

Slipping out of bed, she tiptoed to the door, and trying to be as quiet as possible pattered to the bathroom hoping there would be some aspirins in the medical cabinet there. Her need for aspirin was urgent as she reached up to the cabinet, the agony in her gum driving out her sense of caution—never had she known such pain! Holding a tumbler under the tap, a bottle of aspirin resting in the wash basin, Tiffany went to turn off the tap and felt the glass slipping from her hand. She held her breath as it clattered noisily around the white porcelain, and made a hasty grab to stay its noise. She listened—silence. Thank heaven she hadn't woken Ben. Congratulating herself that the glass was still in one piece, the flat quiet once more, she nearly jumped out of her skin to hear a sound behind her. Whipping round, she saw Ben raking his fingers back through his hair as he came close.

'I've got toothache,' she said woefully, by way of an apology for waking him.

Ben sized up the situation right away, his eyes taking in the bottle of aspirin, the glass in her hand and Tiffany's eyes wide and haunted with pain as she looked at him.

'Get into bed, I'll mix these for you,' he said kindly, all ill will forgotten.

It wasn't until she was back in her room that Tiffany realised she hadn't bothered to put on her robe. At any other time she would have gone scarlet with embarrassment, but her toothache had forced modesty into the background.

Barely had she got into bed when Ben was standing over her. He handed her a glass of the soluble aspirin and she downed it quickly. She saw him glance at the engagement ring on her finger and didn't know whether she was glad or sorry she had gone to bed wearing it. All she knew was that her whole jaw hurt and she was having a hard time in keeping him from knowing the misery she was feeling. 'Thank you,' she murmured as Ben took the glass from her. She wanted him to go—needed the comfort of him with her, but couldn't bear him to see her in this state of weakness.

'Poor baby,' he said gently, pulling the covers up over her shoulders. 'Try and relax.' She felt his hand smoothing the hair back from her forehead, his hand so soothing. Was he undecided about something or was it her overstretched imagination? His voice was gentle still as he asked, 'Shall I leave your small light on?'

'Yes, please.'

When he left her Tiffany tried to relax as he had instructed, tried to sleep, but it was no use. At half past one she was again sitting up, her mind darting desperately from one cure to another she had heard of for toothache. She even picked up a book and tried to read, but it was impossible.

Getting out of bed, she dragged on her robe and stole silently to the kitchen, closing the door noiselessly behind her. There she mixed a salt water rinse and found it helped—for all of two seconds. Ten minutes and a dozen salt water rinses later, she came to the conclusion that salt water was not the answer.

She was siting dejectedly on the settee a few minutes later, rubbing her aching gums with whisky from a glass in front of her, when Ben found her. He took one look at her, saw her eyes were large and unhappy, noted her distressed condition and came to a decision.

'Tiffany,' she looked up at him. 'Tiffany,' he repeated, 'do you trust me?'

She had no idea what this was all about. All she knew was she had never felt so miserable in her life. Her, 'Of course, Ben,' was automatic. Of course she trusted him.

'Right,' he said in a tone that brooked no argument. 'You're coming into my bed with me.' For a full ten seconds Tiffany was unaware of the raging torment in her jaw as she stared at him disbelievingly. 'I've been listening to you roaming around for a quarter of an hour,' he told her, 'and I can't take any more. You're not giving the aspirin a chance to work.' His tone softened. 'Come on, Tiffany, we'll see if Uncle Ben's bed will do the trick.' Then without further ado he was pulling her up from the settee, treating her as a father might.

Only he wasn't her father—he was her husband, Tiffany thought in agony, not knowing which was the worst torture, her toothache or the thought that she was going to be as close to Ben as though she was his proper wife. Once in the room he lost no time putting her into his bed.

'How much whisky have you had?' he asked.

'I'd only just got started,' she mumbled.

'Then I don't think one more aspirin will hurt,' he said half to himself, and left her to return and order her to drink from the glass he held.

When his pyjama-clad body came into the bed beside her, Tiffany tensed, then heard him telling her to relax, telling her she looked about ten years old with her big eyes and mussed-up hair. The shock that had numbed her raging toothache at his suggestion she share his bed had worn off and the gnawing in her jaw was hammering away as hard as ever.

Then suddenly her tenseness left her and with it her independence, and with complete trust in the man lying at her side, she turned to him. It was as though her gesture had proved to him that she knew no harm would befall her, and she felt his comforting arm come round her flimsily covered shoulders as he pulled her towards him. She felt him press her aching jaw into the warmth of his shoulder as with his other hand he pulled the covers up round her, then that hand came beneath the covers to rest lightly on her waist. She heard the security of his, 'All right, poppet?' for all the world as though she was indeed ten years old. Tiffany snuggled her face into his warmth, his strength, and unbelievably the pain in her jaw began to lessen.

When she awoke from an aspirin-induced sleep it was to see the hands of the luminous clock saying it was nearly six.

Ben would have to get up soon, she thought. Then before she could think further on how she had come to be in his bed, she came wide awake with a jolt of shock that hit her senses like a rock plummeting from a high building, as it came to her fully that not only was she in bed with Ben, but that some time during the night, one of his hands had found its way to her breast and the pleasurable warmth she felt in that region was his hand cupping her. For seconds she was unaware of breathing as her body froze and she wondered what to do. If she moved and woke him, he would be equally horrified and it would make his kindly act of last night seem not the pure, clean act of comfort it had been.

Then there was no time or need for her to do anything, for he stirred, seemed to know in his half waking state that she was beside him and moved in closer to her, his hand on her breast closing in a caressing movement, and in that second he seemed to come sharply awake to where he was holding her. A word was quietly strangled from him before she could make out what it was he said, and he had shot out of bed as though the feel of her through her thin nightdress scorched him.

Tiffany's heart steadied when he had gone from the room, and she rolled over into the warm place he had so swiftly vacated. Her toothache was still playing background music, but it was reduced to a bearable pain. She savoured the feeling of being in Ben's bed, knowing that never again would her head rest on his pillow.

She heard him come back into the room, heard his careful opening of drawers so as not to waken her, and stirred, moving back on to her own pillow as though just waking.

'What time is it?' she asked sleepily.

There was a long pause before he told her it was six, then, 'How are you feeling?'

'Much better, thanks.' She sat up switching on the table lamp, as it was not yet daylight and he must be having a difficult time groping around for his things in the dark. 'Thank you for—for looking after me last night.' She saw him more clearly as he came and sat on the edge of the bed. He had a robe on over his pyjamas and she saw the dark shadow of his unshaven chin.

'You'll go to the dentist this morning.' Was he asking her or ordering her? It didn't matter which, she thought as the love she felt for him swelled up within her.

'Oh, yes,' she assured him. 'I couldn't bear another night like last night.' She became confused suddenly. 'The pain, I mean,' then further confused in case he misunderstood, 'Oh,' she said, and blushed furiously, and was rewarded by his grin.

'Do I take it you like being in my bed?' She just couldn't meet his eyes. 'That was an unfair question, wasn't it,' he said, relenting and getting to his feet. 'Do you think a cup of tea would set your tooth off again? Try a lukewarm cup anyway.'

When he had left the flat, Tiffany was in no hurry to leave his bed. They had parted friends, but although she had hoped he might kiss her before he went, he hadn't. Realising if she was to get an emergency appointment with her dentist she would have to be on his doorstep early, she got up.

Her teeth, the dentist said, were perfect, and he had gone on to explain that her sinuses were infected and had affected her upper jaw; a course of antibiotics, she was assured, would cure the trouble. Tiffany could hardly believe him, because it had been a true and agonising toothache she had experienced. But after collecting her prescription from the chemist, she took the large pink tablets as directed and found, much to her surprise, that the dentist had been right in his diagnosis, and that happily, when the time came for her to go back on duty, she was free from pain.

CHAPTER SEVEN

TIFFANY let herself into the flat feeling dull and despondent. It was now nine weeks since she had last seen Ben and she wouldn't be seeing him again this time. She had discreetly found out from the Crewing Office that his flight wasn't due in until Friday, and she would be flying somewhere over the Atlantic by then.

Nine weeks, she recalled, of hopes and fears and disappointment of not once catching a glimpse of him. Was this a foretaste of how she was going to feel when the marriage ended? She turned her thoughts away from that depressing thought. It wouldn't have been so bad if he had left some communication for her. Any sort of note would have done. Even a 'We're out of butter' type of note would have done—anything to indicate that he hadn't forgotten her existence.

During the time since she had last seen him she had done a couple of long haul trips, and after first checking that he wasn't due to arrive in her absence, had spent a few days with her aunt in Middledeane.

Patti Marshall had invited her to her party tonight, but she had refused the invitation, suspecting that since Patti's boy-friend Barry had been the one to introduce her to Nick Cowley, Nick was sure to be there too. It amazed her now to think she had ever thought herself in love with him; she didn't doubt he was deeply involved with her successor by now. Her reasons, though, for not going to the party were not solely because she thought Nick might be there, but also because now that she was married she knew any acceptance would have been accompanied by a feeling of guilt.

But why feel guilty? she argued against her conscience. Hers wasn't a normal marriage, and Ben wouldn't care twopence if she went to a party unescorted. What had they got going for them in their marriage anyway? A few chaste kisses, one night in his bed when he had treated her, for the most part, as if she was a ten-year-old, a handful of companionable moments—if that, and that was all.

Tiffany glanced round the flat—it was immaculate from her ministrations yesterday. There was a fruit cake she had made ready in an airtight tin for when Ben arrived. There was absolutely nothing she could do if she stayed in. She was too restless to want to listen to the radio, nothing she wanted to see on television—why was she making all these excuses? Why not go to Patti's party—other girls went to parties unescorted, didn't they?

She had the phone in her hand and was ringing Patti's number before her conscience could browbeat her into staying at home, and it was too late to back out once she'd heard Patti's delight when she said she would go after all.

'I'm so glad, Tiffany—it will do you a power of good to get out.'

'Oh ...?' What had caused Patti to say that?

'Well, if you don't mind my saying so,' Patti enlightened her, 'I thought you were more quiet than usual this last trip—withdrawn almost.'

That gave Tiffany food for thought. Her pride wouldn't allow her to let other people know she was eating her heart out for Ben, and when the time came to leave for the pub where they were all meeting prior to going on to

Patti's place, attired in the new dress she had bought only yesterday in an attempt to cheer herself up, Tiffany donned it a lighthearted manner that was going to fool anybody who thought she was going into a decline.

It even began to work on her, she thought, when after she had decided to leave her car at home, the taxi dropped her off at the Jolly Brewer. She *was* feeling lighthearted, looking forward to the party, and even giggled at the mad impulse that had urged her to write a note to Ben, and her anticipation of the evening ahead in conversation with some of her friends was in no way lessened as the thought followed that she would be the one to take her note off the mantelpiece when she arrived home, for Ben was still thousands of miles away.

Opening the door of the lounge bar, she was almost deafened by the noise. Most of the party were here already, she saw, spotting Michael Croft obviously telling some risqué story to the three or four men grouped round him. Patti saw her and called her over as a shout of laughter greeted the end of Michael's tale.

'What will you have to drink, Tiffany?' Barry, never far from Patti's side, for all the rough treatment she gave him, asked. Barry wasn't away long and was nearly up to them after coming back from the bar with the iced Cinzano and lemonade Tiffany had said she would like, when Nick Cowley stopped him.

'Have you heard this one?' he began, then seeing Patti from the corner of his eye, said, 'Er—perhaps not, ladies present,' and as his eyes moved further round to catch sight of Tiffany, a surprised exclamation of, 'Tiffy!' broke from him, to be followed by a thorough scrutiny as his eyes travelled over her, taking in her dress of pastel blue crêpe with its fitted crossover bodice and lampshade sleeves flattering her slender arms.

He was trying to get near to her when Patti called, 'Drink up, everybody, let's make tracks for my place. There's plenty to eat, so I suggest we eat first and drink afterwards.' In the general exodus that followed, Tiffany lost sight of Nick, and though he now left her cold, womanlike, she couldn't help being pleased at the admiration she had seen in his eyes.

Tiffany had a lift with Patti and Barry, and another man called Tim, who said he never brought his car when he went to parties. 'Can't afford to with the breathalyser,' he said, going on to tell her he was a sales rep. 'A year's ban on my licence would have me without a job.'

She stayed with Tim for some time after they reached Patti's flat, and only when it dawned on her that he might think she was his partner for the evening did she excuse herself. 'I must circulate a little, Tim. Do you know everyone here?' Apparently he didn't, so she took him and introduced him to several people, and then headed for the kitchen.

The kitchen was empty and there her pose of enjoying herself deserted her. That's just how I feel, she thought. Empty and lost without Ben. She turned, masking her expression as someone pushed through the kitchen door behind her.

'Hello, Nick.' Strange how she could greet him so calmly, while at one time his very appearance would have made her feel all funny inside.

'I've been looking all over for you.'

'Have you?' She was shocked to find herself analysing his features. Good-looking, certainly, but wasn't his mouth a little slack—odd how she'd never noticed that before.

'You're looking as beautiful as ever, Tiffy.'

'Thank you.'

Nick Cowley wasn't used to anyone being aloof with

him—her cool tones began to annoy him. 'You're not still mad at me, are you?'

'Good heavens, of course not!'

'We could have made sweet music together, Tiffy.'

Only then did she perceive that Nick wasn't holding his liquor as well as he might have done. 'It was never on, Nick,' coolly yet sweetly. 'I'm going to join the others. Nice to have ...'

'Not so fast—I think you and I have some unfinished business to attend to first, don't you?'

Obviously he was going to be tiresome, and she eyed the door anxiously, wondering if she could get through it before he knew she had gone. He followed her glance and caught her roughly by the arm.

'No, you don't. You owe me, Tiffy, and I'm a man who likes payment.'

Tiffany tried to back away from him, but came up against the fridge. She wished desperately that someone would come in, and took her eyes off him long enough to glance at the kitchen door. In that instant Nick pounced on her and as he grabbed hold of her she felt the nauseating closeness of his suffocating, loose wet mouth. Kicking and struggling were useless as he fastened himself to her.

'I've always wanted you,' he breathed hotly, 'and now I'm going to have you.'

Her terrified, 'No, Nick!' rent the air.

And then miraculously she was free. Dazed, shaking uncontrollably, she looked about, bewildered, saw Ben standing over Nick's prostrate form, and as Ben turned his hard-eyed grey look on her, her heart sank. She wanted to die as that merciless gaze raked her dishevelled appearance from head to toe. She wanted to say, Ben, Ben, thank God you're here. She opened her mouth to say the words, but the only words she uttered were:

'I want to be sick.'

Ben half carried her over Nick's prone body flat out on the kitchen floor, and pushed her into the bathroom, leaving her to get on with it.

Gulping for air, Tiffany was sick, and afterwards struggled to sit on the edge of the bath. When she began to feel better, she pulled herself on to her feet, found toothpaste in the bathroom cabinet, and knowing Patti wouldn't mind if she used a squeeze to clear the awful taste in her mouth, felt better when she had wiped the toothpaste round her gums, but she could still feel Nick Cowley's lustful mouth on hers.

'Are you all right in there?' Ben's growl reached her, then not waiting for her answer, he pushed the bathroom door. She found the flint hardness of his eyes difficult to meet, but raised her head bravely at his, 'Ready?' He meant was she ready to go home, of course, and weakly she wondered what he would have done if she said 'No,' but she was feeling too beaten to try it.

'Yes—I'm ready.'

'I explained the mess in the kitchen to your hostess,' he said contemptuously, 'when I told her you were leaving. There's no need to say your goodbyes.'

Tiffany didn't begin to think clearly until Ben had put her into his car and they were on their way home. Her mind wouldn't cope with what he was doing back in England when she had thought him elsewhere, and she gave a groan as she remembered the note she had left in the flat.

She saw Ben give her a swift look as her pained groan reached him, then his foot was pressing hard on the accelerator and they were speeding through the outskirts of London. He needn't feel so anxious about her wellbeing, she thought, she wasn't feeling sick any more. Well, not from that scene in Patti's kitchen at any rate, but at the thought he must have read her stupid note to know where she was. That stupid note that read, 'Dear Ben, Have gone to a party, starting at the Jolly Brewer and then on to Patti Marshall's. Do come if you can.' And she had signed it, 'Your wife, Tiffany'.

She stifled another groan. Thank God it was dark and he couldn't see she was shrivelling up with embarrassment.

He had not spoken since they had left the party, and as they entered the sitting room, Tiffany's glance flew to the mantelpiece. Her note had gone.

'I ... I th-think I'll go straight to bed,' she stammered, raising her eyes to meet two chips of granite that were positively taking her apart.

'I think that's a very good idea.' Ben's voice was expressionless as he took in her ashen face. 'I'll talk to you in the morning,' he said ominously, and left her standing in the middle of the carpet.

Tiffany awakened early and as remembrance hit her, she found it impossible to go back to sleep. Slipping noiselessly out of bed, she donned her fluffy dressing gown and made for the kitchen. Ben was in bed still, but there was no getting away from it, she was going to have to face him some time.

What was he doing home? He was probably exhausted since he must have been flying right up until shortly before he had come to the party—but he wasn't due in until Friday. The kettle boiled and with an absent mind she poured water into the teapot and waited for the tea to brew. Her mind still in turmoil, she poured out tea for herself and wondered if Ben was awake, and if so should she take him in a cup.

Almost of their own volition her feet were at his door,

a cup and saucer in her hand. She tapped lightly, but there was no answer. Silently she went in and stood staring down at him in sleep while conquering an overpowering desire to get into that bed beside him and hold him near. Grappling with her wayward thoughts and with a hand that shook, Tiffany placed the cup and saucer on his bedside table.

She had barely made a sound, but Ben opened his eyes, and she saw him stare at her as though she was someone who had just stepped out of his dream. 'Tiffany,' he said softly. Then as if the sound of his own voice had told him he was no longer dreaming, he came wide awake.

His softly spoken, 'Tiffany', gave her small courage a boost. 'I thought you m-might like a cup of tea.' How trite that sounded when what she wanted to do was beg his forgiveness for dragging him into that awful scene with Nick. She knew instinctively that Ben would find such a scene distasteful in the extreme.

Awake now, Ben sat up and looked at her mockingly. 'Thanks,' he said, and Tiffany, not liking the glint in his eye, turned and fled.

She was on her second cup of tea when he joined her in the kitchen. He refilled his own cup before moving to lean negligently against the sink unit.

'How's the head?' he asked.

'I wasn't drunk, Ben.'

One eyebrow lifted questioning her statement. 'No?' he queried.

Oh, if only she could lose her temper with him it would be some sort of defence. But she was wary of him, she had never seen him in this mood, and with her note read, he held all the aces.

'I had a sip of one drink at the pub, and another at Patti's place.'

'Only two? Tell me,' he said almost conversationally, 'are

you usually ill on just two drinks?' Tiffany didn't trust his tone. She wasn't sure, but thought there lurked a violent anger beneath his calm.

'You know what made me sick,' she protested.

'Surely your lover's passion doesn't make you throw up?'

She knew with dead certainty from the way he said that that Ben Maxwell was flamingly angry. He was standing away from the sink now, his body taut, his brow looking like thunder.

'He's not my lover,' she denied quickly.

'You're in love with him.' Tiffany refused to answer, hoping his anger would burn itself out. 'You knew before you went to this party that Cowley would be there,' he accused.

'I . . . I thought he might be.'

'So you wanted to see him.'

'I did not!'

'Why go, then?'

How could she explain? How could she tell this angry man that he was the only man she loved, that it had been go to the party or go mad chasing her thoughts round wondering if he even liked her, let alone loved her?

'You did want to see him,' Ben contradicted her, and went on remorselessly, 'You wanted to feel his arms around you, but when that happened and things looked like getting out of hand, you got scared.' His anger was biting into her. 'Am I right?' he demanded.

He was so wrong, his fury was terrifying, and she could only stare wordlessly at him. She knew she should try and say something to take the heat out of him, but felt in his present mood he wasn't ready to believe anything other than his own interpretation of what he had seen. Her continued silence seemed to annoy him further, and she jumped, her heart thudding madly when he moved towards her, his hand coming down heavily on her shoulders, his grip so strong she was powerless to move. She tried to pull away as she saw the smouldering inferno in his eyes, but her efforts were no match for his strength, and for the first time in her life she knew the panic of outright fear.

'Let me go, Ben,' she pleaded.

'Does passion frighten you, Tiffany?' he asked, while he still had the last remnants of control, and as he felt her tremble in his hold, he said, 'Then I think it's about time you had something to be frightened about.' and his head came down, one hand coming up to clamp her head still as she moved it from side to side trying to get out of his range.

She pushed against him with all her might, but her strength was vastly inferior and his mouth found the target he was seeking. There was nothing in any way chaste as he ravaged her lips, his mouth hard and demanding. Tiffany knew then that he was going to stop at nothing short of her complete surrender. She felt his hand at the back of her head, forcing her mouth against his, and fought as much as she was able when he moved with her and she found herself against the kitchen wall. Then the iron bar of the arm that bound her to him moved and while his lips still demanded her compliance, she felt his hand at her robe, untying it. His hand left her head and then both his arms were encircling her nylon-clad body, the feel of her warmth stoking the passionate fire burning inside him.

Her protest of, 'No—Ben—please!' went unheard as his mouth left hers and he sought the hollows of her shoulders, his inflamed anger ignoring her pleas as her nightdress was ripped away and his mouth found the swell of her breasts. Tiffany felt the touch of his hands moving over her, against her will arousing in her an answering passion she found bewildering because she had never wanted it to be like this, and though she tried to deny her own awakening, when his lips again claimed hers his hands forcing her against his hard body, she could no longer fight the primitive urges he had aroused. Unable to stop herself, she wound her arms up and around him and pressed against his virile body. She was lost completely, unaware of his triumph at her capitulation, and was beyond comprehensive thought when he pushed her away from him.

Her arms were still fastened over his shoulders, her hands clasped at the back of his neck, and only when he took hold of her wrists and dragged her arms away from him did it make itself known that having demonstrated the passion he had said she was so afraid of, having bent her will to his, he had no further use for his experiment.

Hot colour surged through her face and she didn't know anything any more except that she wanted to crawl away somewhere and die, when Ben said, 'For God's sake, girl, cover yourself up,' as though he was now loath to touch her. His words were ragged, and she realised then that while he had found sufficient control to break the passion that had been between them, that control was hanging by a very narrow thread.

Mutely her eyes followed his burning gaze, and she saw, with a return of searing colour, what he could see— the curves of her body still taut with the passion he had aroused, her breasts rising and falling with each raw breath, barely concealed in the torn fragments of her nightdress. Looking away from her body, she saw a nerve banging away in his temple and was incapable of any movement until his ragged voice came to her again.

'For your own sake, Tiffany, take yourself out of my sight—fast!'

At his words and the meaning behind them, the shocked

immobility that had her locked in its grip disappeared, and she went. Shaking from head to foot, she reached her room, barely able to recognise the person she thought she was in the person who had felt those riotous emotions only minutes before, and God help her, she hadn't wanted to leave him. Had he taken her, as she was sure had been in his mind, at that moment she would have given herself willingly.

She sat on her bed waiting for her shaking to cease and had no idea how long she sat nursing her arms about her. But gradually she began to feel calmer and with the return of her other senses she sought for a reason why Ben should reject her when it had seemed at the start that nothing would stop him from what he meant to achieve. With the return of her common sense she realised she didn't have to think too deeply, for while she had been too far gone to count the cost, some part of Ben's mind had not been so deeply committed, and it came to her that very soon now his father would be well again, and when that time came Ben would want to be free to get his annulment. Had he carried out his inclinations an annulment would be out of the question, and although she wasn't very sure on the next point, she had an idea that one had to be married for two years before divorce proceedings could be instigated.

Movement in the next room indicated that she could go and have her shower without the fear of bumping into him. She wasn't ready to face him yet, needed to have some measure of control when next she saw him. Luck was with her and she returned to her room to dress in a cream dress of fine wool. It had classic lines and fitted her perfectly. It helped to boost her rocky confidence to know that outwardly at least she looked cool and slightly remote. But it took all of her courage to leave her bedroom and turn the handle of the sitting room door.

Ben was there as she thought he must be, for all had been quiet in the room next door when she had returned from her ablutions. His hair was still damp from his shower and he was clean-shaven, dressed in dark trousers and white polo-necked sweater. He stood up as she came into the room.

'Come and sit down, Tiffany—we'll talk this thing out.'

His voice was perfectly controlled, causing her to wonder if this was the same man who only a short time ago had been flushed with the dark tide of passion. Was this the same man whose very kisses had taken her to such peaks of ecstasy only to let her fall, her longing for him unfulfilled? And now he wanted to 'Talk this thing out'! She should have known, of course—Ben Maxwell was the sort of man to scorn having any sweepings under the carpet.

She crossed the room and sat down on the settee and Ben reseated himself in the chair he had been sitting in before she had entered.

'I can't apologise for what happened,' he said, coming straight to the point, 'because given the same set of circumstances, I would probably do the same thing again. What I will apologise for, though, is for half scaring you out of your wits, and for that I am sorry.'

Tiffany let his apology sink in, trying to evaluate what in effect he was saying. Was he saying he was putting her response down to the fact that he had frightened her so much her brain had seized up so that he thought she didn't know what she was doing? She felt relief well up within her at that thought, and thought better than to tell him that had it been any man other than him holding her, nothing could have made her respond.

'Y-You were angry because you thought I was enjoying— er—what Nick was doing?' she asked, and receiving no reply reasoned for herself that it didn't matter a jot to him who kissed her, but while she bore his name he would expect more loyalty from her than what he thought he had witnessed last night. 'You were angry because you thought someone else might have come in and seen me in Nick's arms,' she said, sure now that was the reason for his fury. Ben was well respected at Coronet, and if he hadn't flattened Nick and dragged her away from the party, word would soon be buzzing round the Airline that he was a cuckold. His action would leave no doubt if word got out and it was talked about, that you only chatted up Tiffany Maxwell if you were anxious to receive a near broken jaw.

'Angry is putting it mildly,' he said, not answering her question into his reason for knocking Nick down. 'To put it bluntly, I was as mad as hell when I saw that oaf trying to devour you last night—I felt like doing you both a mischief.' The dark look on his face lightened momentarily as though he was reliving the satisfaction of knocking Nick Cowley senseless. 'I would have sorted the matter out with you last night, but ...'

'I wasn't drunk, Ben,' she broke in. 'When I was a child I used to be physically sick after one of my parents' more heated arguments—I d-don't seem to have grown out of it,' she added lamely, while wondering where the nausea was that should have gripped her after Ben had sent her scurrying. She looked at him, saw he was considering her words, and saw him nod as though he believed her. 'Actually,' she confessed in a rush, 'I wasn't going to go to Patti's party, but—well, I'd done all the jobs I could think of to do here, and—well, I was a bit fed up. It's the first time I've been to a party since our wedding.' She didn't want to tell him more than that, and saw with relief that she didn't have to as a look of understanding crossed his face.

'It's not much of a life for you, is it?' he commented.

'Working hard when you're on duty and then not having any fun in your free time. I know it's difficult for you,' he went on slowly, 'but if you can put up with it for a little while longer, I'm sure our present situation will resolve itself to my satisfaction and, I sincerely hope, to yours.'

All the relief she had felt at his understanding vanished at his last words. Was he hinting that their marriage would soon be over? He must be, for he had said 'our present situation will resolve itself to my satisfaction', and as he had never meant their marriage to be anything but temporary, he must now be looking forward to its termination. Following on from that thought, she reasoned his father must be almost well again now.

'How is your father?' she asked, before realising that since Ben couldn't read into her thoughts he must think her to have a grasshopper mind.

He looked at her, paused to catch up with her, then seemed to make the connection, for he said, 'Quite well. In fact he's been home for over a week.' Tiffany wanted Harvey Maxwell to be well and quickly, but her pleasure on hearing he had left the hospital in Switzerland was somewhat dimmed by the knowledge that any time at all now Ben would be putting the wheels in motion for the annulment. She tried to keep her face an aloof mask, but knew it hadn't come off when he leaned forward and said, 'Trust me, Tiffany.'

'Of course I trust you, Ben, you know that,' she said brightly, determined he shouldn't know anything of her bleak thoughts, then went crimson as she remembered the last time she had told him she trusted him, she had spent the night in his bed. The whole atmosphere lightened suddenly as she caught a glimpse of a wicked expression in his eyes as he gathered the reason for her blush. Deliberately she changed the subject.

'How come you're home, anyway? I didn't think you were due in until Friday.' Oh God, she thought, growing more confused, every time I open my mouth I reveal my interest in him; he would know without a doubt now that she had checked with the Crewing Office on his flight plan.

'I was in Vancouver when I heard that Woody Carpenter had gone down with a twenty-four-hour bug of some sort. I offered to take his flight which was due out the next day, and he stayed on in my place, which should give him another couple of days to get over it.' Tiffany suddenly remembered the note she had left, but cancelled any panic by thinking he wouldn't mention it. She was mistaken. 'So I arrived home early. Thanks for your note, by the way,' and as her colour increased, he said just one word: 'Why?'

Tiffany moistened her lips. 'I—er—I suppose it was a bit silly—but I get—I thought—well ...' She knew she was floundering, and her head came up defiantly. 'I thought it would be a nice welcome home.' There, she had just confirmed she was an idiot—leaving him a note when she wasn't even expecting him. She waited for his sarcasm, and was surprised when it didn't come.

'Thank you,' he said quietly. She dared not look at him, but was glad he kept his thoughts on her stupidity to himself, and when he spoke again it was of something entirely different. 'I hope you don't mind, but now the Easter rush is over, I've arranged for you to have a few days off.'

'How do you mean?' she asked, her eyes growing wide. 'I have to report on Thursday.' Without really believing it, she saw a smile break across his face, a smile that turned into a grin that had so much charm in it at having to confess what he had been up to, it took all thought from her head.

'You go back on Sunday,' he corrected her, and went on, seeing in her face that she couldn't believe he had got round the powers that be so easily, 'I told Crewing Officer we wanted time off together, and seeing that we haven't been married all that long, he seemed to think it a good idea.' Then out of politeness since it was *fait accompli* and there wasn't a thing she could do about it, 'Do you mind?'

Tiffany just had to laugh, and it was music in her ears to hear Ben join in. 'I thought we would go and see my father and from there your aunt.'

Secretly Tiffany was delighted. The chance of spending a few days with him, even if those days were to be spent with his father and her aunt, was heaven-sent. Bottling down her exultation, she answered evenly, 'I think that would be rather nice.'

Three hours later they were driving through the leafy lanes of Warwickshire. The countryside was beautiful at this time of the year, trees and hedgerows bursting into life, a variety of greens singing at being released from winter bondage. The sight of several desolate elm trees, once beautiful but now dead after an onslaught from Dutch elm disease, was a sobering sight, but other trees flourished, refusing to be daunted by the death of their neighbours.

The village where Ben's father lived rose just over the Warwickshire border, a quiet village in Worcestershire. Tiffany hadn't realised it was so close to her aunt's. Ben had never discussed his home with her, so she was quite unprepared for the splendour of the old Georgian house that stood waiting for them. Her eyes widened with disbelief when Ben nosed the car through the tall iron gates and up the long drive, and he said, 'Here we are.'

'Ben!' Further words were beyond her.

'Like it?' he asked, his pride in his home barely concealed.

'It's beautiful,' she breathed, and Michael Croft's words came back to her, 'Ben Maxwell could buy Nick's father out any time he wants to'. 'I had no idea you came from this sort of background,' she said. The gardens themselves as they had passed had told her it would cost a great deal in gardeners' wages alone for their upkeep.

'I know you didn't marry me for my money,' Ben said lightly. 'Now close your mouth, you're gaping.'

Both Frances and Harvey Maxwell came out to greet them as they got out of the car, and among the general greetings Tiffany had time to get over her shocked surprise. Then they were stepping into a wide hall and into a room Tiffany took to be the sitting room, uncluttered and cosy despite its high ceiling. A comfortable three-piece suite was grouped round a stone fireplace in which a huge log fire was ablaze.

Father and son studied each other, Ben's eyes keen for any sign of his father's former illness. There was none. 'You look great,' he said quietly. 'It's good to see you back home.' There was emotion in the air and Ben turned to Frances to relieve it. 'But I expect Fran has told you that already.'

Frances agreed she had and smiled at her husband, who returned her smile before he said to Ben, 'Now that I'm home, Ben, and you're here, we must get it all sorted out.'

What it was that was to be sorted out, Tiffany didn't have time to guess, for Frances was saying, 'Come on, Tiffany, we'll leave this pair and I'll show you your room.'

There was no mistaking the joy within Frances Maxwell. It was clear for all to see how happy she was to have her husband back with her. Tiffany felt some of her happiness brushing off on to her and remarked how pleased she was he had made such a good recovery.

'It is marvellous, isn't it—you have no idea how much I missed him while he was away. I wanted to stay in Switzerland with him during his illness, but he wouldn't have it.' Clearly Harvey Maxwell meant everything to her, and suddenly Frances gave a half embarrassed laugh. 'Sorry if I sound a bit soppy,' she said, 'but you have to admit these Maxwell men certainly have that something extra!' Tiffany was able to return her smile without comment; she couldn't with any truth argue against what Frances had said.

The bedroom she showed her to was on the first floor. 'This used to be Ben's room before he left home. We thought you would like to have it during your stay.' For a brief while Tiffany lost some of what else Frances was saying, and came to to hear her say, '... and the bathroom is just across the hall. I'll leave you now to come down when you're ready. Lunch won't be long.'

Tiffany managed to keep her feelings hidden while Frances had been with her, but as soon as she had gone her knees buckled and she sank down heavily on one of the twin beds. Then restlessly she got up again. Yes, both beds had been made up, and unless she'd got it wrong, she and Ben would be sharing this room.

Impossible to make a fuss. Until Ben said otherwise, it was still important that Harvey Maxwell think their marriage a normal one. And had their marriage been normal then she would have been upset if Frances had given them separate rooms. No, she mustn't make a fuss. What was the difference anyway? She had slept in the flat alone with Ben many times—had even slept in his bed and come to no harm!—But, a voice within her argued, that had been before he had aroused her dormant desires this morning.

She was looking sightlessly out of the window when a movement behind her told her Ben had come into the room. She heard a movement like the sound of their cases being put down but didn't turn round, her conviction becoming a certainty that tonight they would be sleeping in the same room. She heard him move coming closer to her, held herself stiff when his hands descended on her shoulders and couldn't relax no matter how hard she tried.

'I should have thought of this,' he apologised, his voice sounding concerned, 'but I didn't.'

Who could resist the concern in his voice? How could she be upset when clearly Ben was hating himself for his lack of foresight? Tiffany's anxiety dissolved, but she could not turn round.

'I didn't think of it either,' she said softly, and because she couldn't bear that because of her he should be made to feel uncomfortable, she said lightly, 'We'll just have to imagine we're at home with a wall between us.' She gave a nervous laugh, and felt the hands of her shoulders tighten, then heard his voice coming huskily to her:

'Do you know something, Tiffany Rowley-Maxwell? I like you.'

She laughed gently because it pleased her that he liked her, and as his hands fell away from her, so too did any tension between them. She turned and moved away from him, her eyes going to her suitcase. 'By the way, Ben Maxwell,' she said, still on a light note, 'you might have told me you were one of the landed gentry.'

'Hardly that,' he replied, that half smile she loved so much in evidence. 'I'll take you a walk round the estate later. Meantime I've come to collect you to take you down for a drink. You were up here so long that your father-in-law is getting impatient to see you.'

She wasn't sure of the truth of that statement, but it didn't matter. She and Ben were friends again, and what was more, he had grown to like her. If only a little love could spring from that liking ... Quickly she preceded him from the room, knowing she must be thankful for what she had.

CHAPTER EIGHT

THEY must have walked miles that afternoon, she and Ben, and by the time they turned back towards the house Tiffany was thoroughly enthralled with everything. They had finished up in the office where Ben had introduced her to Caleb Gibbs, a man in his fifties who had helped with the running of the estate for many years. It was clear as Caleb told her of the paper work involved that the estate was run along business lines, and he added, 'I seem to spend more time in the office than out of it,' talking on, 'not that I mind so much—I'll let the youngsters learn all about the wet and cold of winter!'

They were walking up the drive when she saw a green sports car parked in front of the house, and as she and Ben went into the hall sounds of laughter greeted them from the sitting room. It was with surprise and pleasure that on entering the room, Tiffany saw Holly Barrington.

'Couldn't resist coming over as soon as I knew you two were here,' she greeted Tiffany, and then with typical Holly enthusiasm she launched herself at Ben, kissing him soundly.

'You don't change, Holly,' he told her, 'even though you know I'm a respectable married man.' That pleased Tiffany so much she joined in the rest of the laughter.

Holly said she wasn't staying, for all it was two hours before she departed. 'I've promised Mother I'll be in to-night—she doesn't believe me, of course. No, honestly,' at Frances' invitation that she should stay to dinner, 'I must have an evening at home. Already there are dark mutterings of "I'm sure I've seen your face somewhere before" whenever I go in.'

Holly was incorrigible, Tiffany thought as she sat putting the finishing touches to her make-up prior to going down to dinner that evening. She felt she could have made a true friend of her.

Ben had changed first and had gone down, and she was almost ready herself apart from dropping the long flame-coloured dress over her head. She studied her face in the mirror. Was it too thin? Too fat? In actual fact it was rather a lovely shaped face, but at that moment she was trying to decide which type appealed to Ben. She had long ago discounted that Holly held any interest for him other than affection grown over the years, and Frances' appeal hadn't been the sort to hold his attention for very long, so what type of girl did he go for? She had never heard of him dating any of the stewardesses, but in Switzerland Holly had mentioned a Paula somebody or other and a Karen who had made him disappear in the opposite direction—she didn't know if they were dark-haired like herself or redheads or even blonde.

The unexpected turning of the door handle made her jump and had her looking frantically round for her robe, but Ben was already in the room, his glance flicking over her seated in her petti-bra at the dressing table.

'Sorry, Tiffany,' he said, the door closed behind him. 'I can't back out, my father's in the corridor,' and then to try and lighten the confused look of her, 'My, you're a pretty pink!'

'I—I should have been ready,' she told him, leaving her seat and taking her dress from its hanger, 'but it's so peaceful here I somehow lost all sense of time.'

She had her dress half over her head when she heard him say, 'You like it here?' and straightening up after pulling the folds of her dress into place, she found his eyes fixed on her, and for an instant thought he looked as if her answer was important to him, then he smiled and she knew she had imagined it.

'Yes, I do,' she answered, and wanted to tell him that in a very short space of time she had come to love Linwood, but was afraid he might see she loved him too. 'I like it,' she understated, but she thought he knew she was sincere because there was an element of warmth creeping into his smile.

She looked away from him as she struggled with her zip, and found herself spun round, felt his hands fixing it for her, making her feel a delicious tingle as his fingers came into contact with her warm skin.

'My father wants me to come down and take over from him,' he said, his task completed as Tiffany turned round to stare at him.

'Do you mean—come and live here?' Her throat felt dry, she couldn't take it in for a minute, and to hide the gamut of emotions at what that would mean, she returned to the dressing table and picked up her lipstick.

'What with his illness and his refusal to have Fran join him in Switzerland, one way and another they got off to a very bad start, so they've decided to go on an extended honeymoon. Dad says the estate is too much for him now, and since it will be mine one day anyway, he's only waiting until I can take over before he and Fran get off.'

Tiffany couldn't say that what he had just told her was anything other than an enormous jolt, and she was never more glad than to be able to summon up her pride as her eyes met his in the mirror. There seemed to be a question lurking in the depths of those grey eyes, but she had no way of knowing what it was. Was he telling her that as soon as the arrangements for him to take over had been completed their marriage would be at an end? She didn't know, but pride was forcing her to be casual.

'You don't mind leaving the Airline?'

If he was put out by her casually asked question, he certainly covered it well, she thought. 'No, I shan't mind—I've enjoyed the life, but I've always known it wasn't permanent. My contract runs out at the end of the summer—I won't be renewing it.' He was about to add something else when a maid tapped on the door to say dinner was almost ready.

Should she ask him about the annulment or wait for him to mention it? Tiffany wondered as she went with him down the stairs. And because she couldn't bear to think about it, let alone bring the matter up, she decided to leave it all to him. Perhaps she was being weak, she conceded, but where he was concerned she didn't want to think further than today. She would enjoy the remainder of the time she had left with him, she resolved, and tomorrow would be faced when it came.

Talk over dinner touched on Ben taking over the estate, but was mainly about the places Frances and Harvey hoped to visit. It was a strange evening for Tiffany. It was as if now, knowing that the break between her and Ben would come with the ending of summer, each moment was precious, moments to be stored for when he had gone out of her life for ever. She concentrated on enjoying the evening, on not fretting or worrying, on making sure no note of discord touched them, and found with surprise that she had laughed quite naturally when anyone said anything amusing, and when she and Ben said goodnight to Frances and Harvey she realised it was one of the best evenings she had ever spent.

Her feeling of goodwill lasted until she and Ben were in the bedroom they were to share, then an embarrassed shyness came over her, threatening to freeze her over. She couldn't undress with Ben in the same room, she just couldn't. Yet to be seen coming back from the bathroom by either Fran or Harvey with a bundle of clothes under her arm, and wondering what they would make of that, was not to be thought of.

'Something wrong?' Ben had already taken off his jacket, and attracted by the very stillness of her was looking across, the expression on her face halting him as he began to undo his cuff links. 'You're not worried I might act like I did first thing this morning, are you?' he asked, his face suddenly sombre as he mistook her embarrassed shyness for fear. 'Rape isn't quite in my line.' She could hear an edge creeping into his voice. 'And I don't intend to start with my wife.'

'It isn't that,' Tiffany said quickly.

'Then what the hell's causing you to look like that?' he exploded. 'If you're not all knotted up with the fear we shall be using only one bed tonight, what in God's name is wrong with you?'

His stinging tone was doing nothing to make her feel less of a fool. He was making her feel more stupid than ever, and the longer she delayed in telling him, the greater it became in magnitude. Then suddenly he seemed to realise it wasn't fear that kept her mute, seemed to recognise at last that she was almost going under with the weight of embarrassment, and he came over to her, his fingers lifting her chin with a gentle touch until he was looking down into her velvety brown eyes.

'Come on, poppet—surely you can tell me what's wrong?'

That 'poppet' put everything back into perspective, and it didn't matter that he was treating her like the same child he had that night he had taken her into his bed, her throat unlocked.

'I c-can't undress with you here,' she whispered.

A spurt of anger helped her at his ear-splitting grin. She didn't doubt then that he was regularly in the habit of stripping off in front of a chosen member of the opposite sex, but she had never done it before, and even married to him, she couldn't do it now.

'Oh, Tiffany—you baby!' didn't help matters, and she jerked her chin out of his grasp only to feel his arms come around her in a loose hold. 'How about if I disappear to the bathroom while you undress and get into that old faithful thing you call a dressing gown? Then when I come back you can go and clean your teeth and by the time you return I should be in bed.' He cocked his head to one side, laughter not very far away she was sure, for all he adopted a serious look. 'Well, what do you think of my master plan?'

To think that six months ago she had thought Ben Maxwell an iceberg of a man! She had thought him so cold, ruthless, tiresome and belligerent, and now he was so dear to her, so infinitely lovable. Her anger evaporated and a smile she couldn't stay winged its way to him. His arms dropped away from her as her smile hit him, and he turned away muttering something about finding his toothbrush.

Coming back from the bathroom donned in her 'old faithful', she realised everything had gone according to plan except that Ben was not in his bed as he should have been, but was standing with a robe over his pyjamas, poking through her paraphernalia on the dressing table.

'What's this for?' he asked, holding up a short-bristled brush.

'It's for putting on blusher,' she answered, only just resisting the impulse to grab it out of his hand.

'I shouldn't have thought you had any need of it,' he

offered, and if that was an oblique reference to the way it seemed to her he had her blushing every five minutes, she chose to ignore it.

'I don't use it all that often.' She strove for a casual note, but her tummy flipped when she saw his grin appear. And since he was still occupied poking through her things on the dressing table, she took advantage of his turned back and was in bed by the time he had finished his inspection.

'Sir Frank Whittle could have learned a thing or two from you,' he remarked.

Tiffany was smiling as she turned her head away from him on her pillow. Sir Frank Whittle, she remembered, had been one of the pioneers in the invention of the jet engine —an engine that had assisted the jet plane to move faster than sound.

She heard the other bed give beneath Ben's weight. 'Are you going to read or shall I put out the light?' his voice came quiet, matter-of-fact.

'I—I think I'm ready for sleep.'

The light went out. She heard more movement as he lay down. She had her back to him and prayed that sleep would come quickly; this was going to be a night of agony if she couldn't forget he was so close yet so far.

'Goodnight,' she said, and was ashamed of the huskiness that penetrated her voice.

It was her imagination, of course, pure imagination, that had her hearing an answering husky note as Ben said, 'Goodnight, Tiffany.'

She awoke to a glorious May morning to hear the birds singing, telling her how good it was to be alive. Extending her arms above her head, she stretched deliciously. She had slept well even though it had seemed like hours before sleep had finally claimed her.

Lying on her back, she stared up at the ceiling. She

wouldn't look at the other bed yet. Ben had probably been up ages even though without looking at her watch she knew it was still quite early. It was too lovely a day to waste in bed, but how heavenly to be able to lie here in the peace that surrounded Linwood and not to have to dash around getting ready to go to the airport. Funny, that—no matter how early she got up, it was always a last-minute dash to be at work on time.

'Are you determined not to look this way?' Tiffany's head shot round as Ben's voice shattered the calm of her thoughts to see him propped up on one elbow taking his fill of her. 'I've been waiting to say good morning to you —you've been awake ten minutes.'

Exaggeration, of course, but Ben didn't appear to be in the slightest perturbed by their enforced propinquity; she wished she could say the same for herself. She tried for the same casual note he had used, as she smiled an offhand, 'Good morning.'

His shout of laughter confirmed that her 'Good morning' had been too casual, and she turned her head away as he whipped back his covers and got out of bed. 'You can look now,' his voice tormented her, and she was forced to match his amusement when she looked back and saw him tying the belt of his robe.

Her heart beat a rapid tattoo when he calmly told her to move over and came to sit on the edge of her bed. 'I shall have to leave you to your own devices for most of the day,' he informed her. 'There are a few things I have to go into connected with the estate—I'm sorry, but it's necessary.'

'I don't mind,' Tiffany told him, but she did mind, a whole lot. She wanted Ben to herself and while freely admitting she was being selfish, she excused herself that all too soon there would be no Ben in her life.

As Frances too was at a loose end once the two men had

departed for the study, she suggested she and Tiffany go shopping, and when Tiffany agreed that it was a good idea, Frances said, 'Do you think they'll shoot us if we interrupt them to tell them where we're going?' Tiffany followed her into the study, where Frances announced, 'We're going on a spending spree.'

'Have you enough money with you, Tiffany?' Ben asked, his hand going to his wallet pocket.

Tiffany froze. She didn't want Ben's money. She heard Harvey saying to Frances, 'I expect you could do with some loose change too, couldn't you, my dear,' but Tiffany was concentrating more on making certain she didn't have to take the notes Ben was pushing her way.

'No!' she said, more sharply than she meant to, and found herself hauled up against him with his arms round her as he turned her where his father, engaged in talking to Frances, could not see her face.

'For God's sake,' Ben's voice grated in her ear, 'do you want to give the game away?' She felt sure he would have shaken her had they been alone. As it was, to the on-looker it would appear as though he was taking this op-portunity to give his bride of a few months a very thorough hug before she went on her way. Tiffany heard his harsh, 'If my money offends you so much you can give it back later —but for now you're damn well going to take it!'

Unbending, Tiffany stood stiffly in his arms. She knew he wasn't going to let her go until she agreed. 'All right,' she said.

Thankful that Frances was unaware of the tension she was feeling as they drove into town, Tiffany cursed herself for the independent streak in her that made it impossible for her to accept money from Ben. She knew without dwelling on it that she had spoilt things between them—they had been getting on so well too.

She gave up chasing her thoughts around in circles and concentrated her attention on Frances' guided tour of the town, and once she had pushed her despair into the background, although not the same as being with Ben, she was able to extract some pleasure from the expedition. Not that they bought very much, but by the time they were ready to return to Linwood she felt more able to face him again.

Returning the money to him was made easy by Frances returning most of her money to Harvey with a light, 'Keep that for me, darling, I didn't see anything I wanted today,' and she laughed as she added, 'But I probably shall the next time I go into town!'

Tiffany handed Ben's money back with a similar, 'Most frustrating, but ...' Ben received the notes without comment.

After dinner that night Frances confessed to feeling a little tired. 'We must have ploughed miles round the shops today.' Tiffany agreed and had the perfect opportunity of asking if anyone would mind if she had an early night. Whatever happened, she couldn't go through the same ritual of getting into bed as last night. With a bit of luck, if she went to bed now, by the time Ben came up she would be asleep.

She wasn't, of course. Frances and Harvey had come up soon after her, but it must have been a couple of hours later before the bedroom door was quietly opened and closed. She willed herself to keep her breathing even, and heard Ben moving around, quietly for such a big man.

When she dared a quick glance across at his bed the following morning it was to see it was empty, and she was glad about that. Ever since that episode in the study yesterday, things had changed between them. She felt she could no longer be natural with him, and the more she tried to counter this mood, the more stiff she felt she came across.

As for Ben, apart from the show he put up in front of Frances and his father, he was unyielding in his attitude towards her.

They were leaving today for Middledeane and much as she loved her aunt, Tiffany felt she would much rather not go. But on reflection she realised it was preferable to have a third person present to returning to the flat and being alone in his company. To think that this time yesterday she had wanted him exclusively to herself, yet now, within the space of twenty-four hours, the idea appalled her.

The journey to Middledeane was completed with barely a word passing between them. Ben seemed preoccupied with his thoughts, and not for anything would Tiffany have tried to start up a conversation with him. He seemed bent on playing Captain Maxwell of Coronet, so let him get on with it! she fumed.

His greeting to her aunt, though, was as warm as it had ever been, underlining to Tiffany that it was just her he was out with.

'Show Ben where to put your cases, Tiffany,' her aunt said, when their greeting were over. 'I've had another bed put into your room just in case you felt a little cramped in your three-quarter bed.'

That was one worry off Tiffany's mind. Her aunt's thoughtfulness to Ben's size meant she wouldn't be sitting up in a chair all night as she had envisaged.

The visit passed without incident, Ben putting in as much effort as herself to ensure that Margery Bradburn was unaware how things really stood between them. Though when they were on their own, there seemed to be a brick wall between them. The strain of keeping her aunt from knowing the true situation began to get Tiffany down. Soon she would have to tell the dear soul that she and Ben were splitting up, and on the last day of their visit she wondered if it was fair to spring it on her at the last minute. Wouldn't it be better to give her some hint?

Deciding against it, Tiffany stood with her aunt while Ben took their cases out to the car, but when Margery Bradburn said, 'You look thoughtful, dear?' Tiffany saw an opportunity to try and break it to her gently.

'Aunty——' she hesitated, then began again urgently before Ben could come back, thinking it wasn't fair, once more, to leave her aunt in this fool's paradise. 'Aunty, I wasn't going to say anything just yet, but,' and she paused only briefly before hurrying on, '... but I have something to tell you ...' The unprepared-for rapture of her aunt's smile stopped her in her tracks, then before she could say more, say anything that would turn that rapturous smile to tears, she felt Ben's arm come round her, his grip biting into her waist.

'Not yet, Tiffany,' he said smoothly, and it was she who was the most mystified of the three of them as they went down the path to the waiting car, her aunt's look seeming to say she understood perfectly that Ben wanted what she had to tell her to be a secret a little while longer.

There was no doubt about it, Ben was furiously angry; she knew the signs even if her aunt was unaware of them. He kept his arm about her waist, looking for all the world like a devoted husband as he handed her into the car and closed the door. Tiffany turned to wave to her aunt as the car turned the corner, then settled back in her seat with a picture of her aunt's beaming face still with her.

She knew Ben was too angry to want to bother talking to her, and resigned herself for a silent drive to London. But once clear of Middledeane he pulled on to a grass verge, cut the engine, and turned towards her. Tiffany knew then that he was ready to pulverise her, if not physically, then with a few none too carefully chosen words. She wasn't disappointed.

'And just what in sweet hell were you going to tell your aunt?' he asked ominously.

'I ...' She could get no further. She had felt the strength of his temper before, but this enraged man leaning over her, his fingers digging into her arms as though suspecting she was about to open the car door to get away from him, was something new. The storm must have been building up inside him ever since Linwood, she realised, and she hastened to find her voice before he lost the small control he had when anything could happen, and by the look of it, murder. 'I w-was—that is, I ...' she tried again, and felt real fear when his hands left her arms to settle round her throat. 'Be reasonable, Ben,' she fought to hide her fear. 'You know m-my aunt is all dewy-eyed over us. She's g-going to be terribly upset wh-when we split up.' The fingers round her throat tightened at her last word, taking the rest of her explanation from her as she gasped, 'Please, Ben—you're choking me!'

Only then did the mists of his rage let up slightly, and he looked at her grim-faced, as he let his hands fall. 'We'll split up when I say so, and not before,' he bit at her. 'God, you make me so mad I could cheerfully throttle you!'

Tiffany didn't think now was the time to tell him he very nearly had. But she saw some of his rage leave him, saw his control returning, but was frightened to say one word in case she triggered it off again. When his voice next came, it was icy with the control he was exerting.

'You realise, of course, that your aunt has gone hurrying to find her knitting pins and white wool.'

'Wh-what do you mean?' She hadn't a clue what tack he was on now.

'Hell's bells, do I have to spell it out for you?' his voice exploded violently, the ice fractured. 'Your aunt is under the impression that you're the radiantly happy wife of a blissfully happy husband.' That illusion would soon be shattered if she could see them now, Tiffany thought, still not with him. 'Now what,' he went on brutally, 'is she expected to think, believing as she does that we're the happiest couple since Adam and Eve, when you tell her you have "something to tell her?" '

Tiffany stared at him blankly. Then hot colour surged through her cheeks. 'You m-mean . . .'

'Exactly,' said Ben through gritted teeth. 'You've just as good as told her you're pregnant.' Oh God, Tiffany thought, feeling as though she was drowning in a whirlpool with no way out. She didn't think she was capable of any other emotion just then but sheer remorse at the pain she would be causing her aunt, but when Ben's next words reached her, rage so powerful stormed through her that it made her totally irresponsible for her actions. 'So,' he jibed, 'since we're now to believe that you're pregnant, and since I don't recall having had the pleasure,' he paused, then said his voice deliberately goading, 'perhaps you'll be good enough to tell me who did?'

All her pent-up emotions of the last few days fused together in one high-powered voltage shot, and without knowing what she was doing, incensed by his jibe, Tiffany's hand arched through the air and she hit him with all of her force, catching him squarely on the side of his face. The sound of it echoed back in the closed car and her eyes widened as she saw a livid mark appear on his cheek, and she just stared wide-eyed, unable to believe as her senses returned that she was responsible for it. She knew for certain that he would choke her now, and as tears coursed silently and unheeded down her cheeks and she waited to meet her fate, she realised with beaten certainty that this was the end of all her hopes for her marriage, and she just didn't care about anything any more.

The shock of the touch of his hands closing over hers as they lay in her lap had her looking wordlessly at him. 'Don't cry,' he said quietly, and only then was she aware of her tears. 'That was a filthy remark and I know completely unfounded.' Tiffany snatched her hands away from him to find her hanky and wipe her eyes. 'I'm most sincerely sorry,' said Ben, and she knew he meant it. But wanting to yield at the remorse in him, probably caused, she thought, by seeing her cry for the first time, Tiffany found she couldn't.

'Let's forget it,' she said woodenly, and turned her face away from him, knowing already that she had forgiven him, was so much in love with him she would forgive him anything, but to find it in her to unbend was an impossibility.

Silence followed her words, and as she refused to look at him, Ben took his hands away from her, his tones sombre as he said, closing the subject, 'You'd better ring your aunt when we get home and invent some other news.'

Though he put his foot down, the drive back to London seemed to Tiffany to be never-ending. She felt utterly spent and in no mood for idle conversation, and Ben too seemed equally used up. She thought his relief was as great as hers when he drew up outside the apartment and they were both free from the incarceration of the car.

Whether things would have simmered down between them, whether they would have found something of the friendly atmosphere that had been with them on the journey down to Linwood before she went on duty tomorrow, Tiffany knew she would never know, for all hopes of an easing of hostilities vanished into the air as Ben looked through the mail that had arrived in their absence.

'One for you,' he said, and actually seemed to be studying the postmark before handing it over to her.

If she had possessed more savoir-faire, she realised later, she would have said 'Thanks' and taken it from him to read another time, but the surprise of seeing Nick Cowley's handwriting when she had given him very little thought since her last unfortunate encounter with him had her uttering a puzzled, 'Nick,' before her scattered wits returned, and looking up from the envelope in her hands, she felt a cold chill as her eyes met hard grey eyes that threatened to pierce straight through her.

'Are you in the habit of receiving letters from your— from him?'

'No, of course not,' she denied.

'He doesn't appear to have had any trouble finding out where you live.' His eyes narrowed threateningly. 'He hasn't been here, has he?' he rapped out.

'Good heavens, no!'

'Make sure he doesn't come here either,' he bit at her darkly.

'What do you take me for? Of course I wouldn't ask him here. You know I . . .' Oh, what was the use? Even if she did tell him the very thought of Nick nauseated her, he wouldn't believe her. The mood he was in now he wouldn't believe anything she told him.

Suddenly she was tired of doing battle with Ben. Tired and weary of this constant warring. And since it took two to make a fight, she turned silently away from him, her letter still in her hand, and walked from him and into her room.

Ben didn't trust her, that much was obvious. He just didn't trust her, and aside from all other considerations, what was a marriage without trust? All her secret hopes that something might come of her marriage to him were dashed to the ground with the realisation of his lack of faith in her. It didn't stop her wanting him—she loved

him and wanted him, full stop, but she didn't want a
marriage that followed the same pattern as her parents', the
same constant bickering—she'd heard enough of that to last
her a lifetime.

She stiffened as Ben came into her room, but remained
where she was sitting on the edge of her bed. She had no
idea what he wanted, but hardly thought he had come in
to try and make friends. Suddenly the room was too small
with Ben in it; he was crowding her and she had to get
away from him, away from the man who tortured her very
soul. She looked up at him, a decision she hadn't looked
for upon her, and entirely without emotion she told him of
that decision.

'I want this marriage ended,' she said calmly. 'I want it
ended—and now.'

CHAPTER NINE

A DREADFUL silence hung in the air at her words. Then Ben
spoke. 'You want our marriage ended—just like that.'

She should have mistrusted the mildness of his tone,
Tiffany realised much later, should have known better than
to think he would accept her decree without question.

'Your decision wouldn't have anything to do with your
letter from lover-boy, would it?' he questioned, making her
gasp—she hadn't even read her letter from Nick yet. Hearing her gasp seemed to clinch it for him that his accusation
had hit the truth. 'So you aren't as immune to him as you
would have me believe?—You didn't require my assistance
at the party,' he said, the thin veneer of his mildness gone

to reveal the red-hot lava of his temper. 'You were in fact merely playing hard to get.'

'No,' broke from Tiffany. 'You've got it all wrong.'

'Like hell I have!' She knew then that nothing she could say to him was going to get through his volcanic rage. 'Well, let me tell you, Mrs Maxwell, you're married to me and that's the way you'll stay ...'

'I will not,' Tiffany broke in, as temper she didn't know she had made her defy him. 'I'm leaving this apartment,' she shouted, 'leaving you, and then I...'

She got no further. Suddenly she was lying down on her bed with the weight of his body holding her down. It happened so quickly, so fast, for a moment she had no idea how she had got there. Then Ben's lips were over hers, hard and ruthless, and she was fighting like a wildcat but finding herself powerless against his strength.

His angry mouth claimed hers again and again while his hands tore at her clothes. The hysterical thought, my God, he's going to rape me, seared like lightning across her brain, but there was no time for panic, it was happening now, no time to decide what to do, but to get in and do it. She felt, heard, the buttons on her shirt snap off as he tore it open, felt one experienced hand come to the back of her, and where she sometimes had difficulty in doing up the stiff fastening of this particular bra, felt it give as he had no difficulty at all in undoing it. Unaware of her shirt being taken from her arms, she was shocked to find the top half of her naked as her bra followed her shirt on to the floor and Ben's hands moulded her breasts, his touch leaving her only for his mouth to plunder where his hands had been.

'No, Ben!' she screamed, and was ignored, felt his hands at the zip of her jeans and heard a ripping sound as they were dragged from her and were tossed in a pile with her other things. Then his mouth was again on hers, punishingly forcing her lips apart.

The worst part of it all, the thought passed dimly through her mind, was that if he didn't stop soon it wouldn't be rape, for he was arousing in her feelings she didn't want, and not only was she fighting against him but against the response she knew she would give him if he didn't soon stop.

She felt the naked warmth of his chest against her breasts and knew his shirt was off, and then, wanting only to yield to him, she knew that Ben with his inherent breeding would find it impossible to live with himself if he took her this way. And for that reason and that reason only, when now her body was begging him to take her, she found enough will power to stop struggling, and when after a few seconds of kissing her lifeless mouth he raised his head, she was able to whisper:

'You'll hate not only me but yourself, afterwards, Ben.'

He looked back at her, and she knew she could have saved herself the effort, because he was going to ignore her. Then a dazed looked came over his face and as if in a trance he stretched out a hand to touch her sad face, only to withdraw it as like someone waking from a bad dream he rolled away from her and stood up. Tiffany covered her breasts with her hands, thankful her brief bikini pants were still covering her, and watched the look of complete disbelief wash over his face as it registered that he had been within a minute of raping his wife, saw the look of disbelief change to self-loathing, self-disgust, and could have wept for him.

'Oh, God Almighty!' was jerked from him, ragged as though he still didn't believe it. Then as though the sight of her distraught face, the red marks on her arms and body that would turn to bruises, were too much for him to cope with together with his thoughts, he turned and left her.

She didn't see Ben again that day—didn't want to. While she thought she was prepared to forgive him, she knew he would have a hard time forgiving himself; that much about him she had learned.

She was in the kitchen the next morning, pale but outwardly composed, hurriedly sipping a cup of tea before dashing off to the airport, when she heard a sound and knew that Ben had joined her.

'We must talk, Tiffany.' His voice sounded perfectly controlled, she thought, and only hoped her voice would sound the same when the time came for her to answer him. 'There's—a lot I want to say to you.' ·

She met his glance steadily, willing herself not to go soft at the sight of him dressed in slacks and sweater, but with a tiredness in his eyes that told her he had slept no better than she had.

'Very well.' She was determined not to let him see how his very presence turned her legs to water. They both knew there was no time for him to tell her anything now if she was to be at the airport on time.

His, 'Tiffany,' arrested her as she was shrugging into her uniform jacket. 'Will you ...' and then with a touch of his old asperity showing through, 'I want you to hold off leaving until we've had a talk.'

She was picking up her bag as she gave him a cool, 'All right, Ben.'

She was still congratulating herself on how cool she had managed to sound when she drove into the staff car park. She had no idea when she would see him again to have their 'talk', but as he was leaving the Airline at the end of the summer it must be soon. What there was to talk about though, for all he had said he had a lot to tell her, she couldn't begin to guess. It was a foregone conclusion that their marriage would end with his contract with Coronet anyway, so why he had become enraged when she had wanted to precipitate it, she couldn't think. He was much too honest a person to prevaricate, so why when she had wanted their marriage to end without delay had he all but ... Tiffany blanked her mind off at that point as she had through the long hours of the night, and decided yet again that Ben's reason for not wanting the annulment to go through just yet was because since he thought she was still in love with Nick Cowley and out of some mistaken sense of chivalry, knowing Nick didn't have marriage in mind, he was trying to protect her. Even that didn't add up, because there was no saying Nick wouldn't be around when she was free. Tiffany gave up trying to puzzle it out; she felt like a dog who had been chasing its tail with the same thoughts whirling round and around in her brain and coming out precisely nowhere.

She was surprised to see Sheila Roberts working in the Crewing Office, and her surprise must have shown, for Sheila told her, 'I'm grounded for a while,' and went on to tell her she had been having earache and had had the mother and father of all nosebleeds. Sheila looked glum. 'So I'm stuck here until I get the O.K. from the specialists.'

Tiffany felt genuine sympathy for her; she couldn't pretend she liked the gossipy girl, but she very much doubted the specialists would give her the all-clear to fly again, for the hours spent in pressurised cabins spelt doom to any stewardess with ear trouble.

As Tiffany anticipated, she had very little time to think of Ben once they were airborne, though she did pause to muse how strange fate was. At one time, when she couldn't stand him, she had seemed to fly with him quite often, but since their marriage she hadn't flown with him once.

She was pleased to see Patti Marshall was one of the stewardesses on this trip, for not only was Patti a good friend, but it gave her a chance to apologise for her abrupt departure from her party.

'That stupid Nick!' Patti said with instant understanding, saving Tiffany from going into an embarrassing explanation. 'It wasn't funny at the time but I get the giggles every time I think of my going into the kitchen and seeing Nick Cowley spreadeagled doing his "where am I?" bit.' Patti burst into a fit of giggles, and Tiffany couldn't help but picture the scene as Patti saw it, and grin with her. Then when Patti had controlled her mirth, she went on to tell her, 'Barry sobered Nick up and gave him a bit of a lecture—I think it made him realise he'd made an ass of himself. Anyway, before he left he said he'd be writing to you to apologise—I gave him your address. Did he write?'

'Y-yes,' Tiffany answered, and realised Patti had read more into her hesitant answer than she had meant her to. 'Ben gave me the letter ...'

'Strewth!' exclaimed Patti before she could finish. 'I never thought of that. He was mad enough to bite nails in half when when he came to say you were going home. Was he very annoyed at Nick writing to you?'

'A bit,' said Tiffany, and as their brief respite ended, she thought that must be the understatement of the decade!

The rest of the trip passed with the usual happenings—someone being airsick, someone having too much to drink—nothing that hadn't happened before, and all taken in the stride of the experienced stewardesses. In no time at all the weeks went by and Tiffany was again in the staff car park. Before getting into her Mini she looked round for Ben's car, spotted it and wondered over which part of the globe he was flying at the moment, and wasn't sure whether she wanted him to arrive back in London before she finished her rest days or not.

She could have found out when he was due in from

Sheila Roberts, but she could just see her passing the news around, 'And imagine, she didn't even know his flight plan!' She did see Sheila for Sheila to tell her that they had been hit by a 'flu epidemic and that most of the stewardesses were on stand-by. That could mean she could be called out at any time to take on someone else's duty.

Tiffany drove home through the summer rain—how soon June had come around! She let herself into the flat, quiet without Ben. Not that he was noisy, but he gave the apartment that lived-in feeling, and she had to confess that much as she loved the apartment, it wasn't the same without him in it.

It was as she went into the sitting room after changing out of her uniform that she saw an envelope propped up against a little porcelain vase on the mantelpiece. In haste she picked it up, and there her haste ended. She was frightened to open it—frightened in case he had had second thoughts about their 'talk' and that his note was saying she would be hearing from his solicitors—perhaps not ever seeing him again.

With trembling fingers she withdrew the single sheet of notepaper, read what he had written once, then again, then promptly burst into tears. 'Dear Tiffany,' he had written in his strong masculine scrawl, 'Welcome home. Ben'.

Tears of relief and happiness streamed down her face. 'Ben, oh, Ben!' she whispered. He would never know how much his simple note meant to her. She forgave him everything as again and again she studied his handwriting, and again and again as she busied herself cleaning an already clean apartment, the words went through her brain, 'Dear Tiffany, Welcome home. Ben'.

The next day she did some shopping. Not that there was a lot she could buy for the store cupboards, as since she had refused a housekeeping allowance, Ben had taken to re-stocking the cupboards himself. But there was the inevitable trip to the cleaners and a few odds and ends she needed.

Returning to the flat, she was greeted by the faint lingering smell of furniture polish as she went through into her bedroom. The flat would be shining when Ben walked in, and she had managed to keep herself fully occupied. She had telephoned Aunt Margery last night and again had felt the compulsion to give her some hint about the break between her and Ben that was bound to come before too long, but something had held her back and she wasn't sure if it was fear of hurting her aunt that had kept her silent or because Ben had wanted her to leave things as they were for the moment.

Thinking about her aunt triggered off the impulse to take out the box containing the white nightdress and matching negligee she had given her. Tiffany shook them out of their folds, her eyes lingering on the feminine garments, knowing she would never wear them. Choked by sudden thoughts of what would never be, she left the froth of white on her bed and went hurriedly into the bathroom where she bathed, washed her hair and bundled herself into her fluffy dressing gown. While her hair was drying, she made herself a sandwich and a cup of coffee, took her snack meal into the sitting room and picking up the paper started on the crossword.

Some time later, stuck on a clue, she went to her room to tidy her hair, brushing it vigorously until it floated and crackled around her head and shoulders. About to leave her room, she caught sight of her aunt's gift draped across the bed, and on a sudden impulse she discarded her well-used dressing gown, and with barely a pause slipped the nightdress over her head, and while the mood was still with her, she then pulled on the matching negligee.

She wouldn't have been female if she had been able to resist the urge to take a look at her reflection in the mirror. Her eyes didn't see the picture of refreshing innocence and unawakened womanhood as brown eyes stared back at her. She saw a slightly pink face, devoid of make-up, her hair floating in shining waves about her shoulders, and a dream of white falling from her shoulders to the ground, her curves obvious but concealed. 'You, my dear,' she told her reflection, 'look quite nice,' then with a half ashamed grin for talking to herself, she went back to her crossword.

Still puzzling on the elusive answer to her crossword clue, Tiffany kicked off her slippers and tucked her feet beneath her on the settee. How warm and peaceful the apartment was. How cosy, she thought dreamily. Where is Ben, I wonder?

She awakened slowly, some subconscious instinct telling her she was not alone. She looked to the door and came tingling awake and alive to see Ben standing with his back to the closed door, his eyes going slowly over her.

Her hair was tousled, her cheeks flushed from sleep, and she had no idea what a delightful picture she made in her bridal attire. All she knew was that she hadn't meant Ben to see her like this, and although she appreciated his warm look, she knew she had to get out of it and fast. She made a move to rise to her feet.

'No, don't get up,' Ben stopped her, his voice sounding a shade thick. Tiffany subsided back on to the settee mainly because as his eyes wandered over her figure and back to her face, she was swamped by such a feeling of wanting to fling herself into his arms, she did not dare do anything that would take her a pace nearer. 'You look beautiful,' he breathed, and moved from the door towards her.

Tiffany just sat and stared at him, feeling suspended in a mindless vacuum. Ben came nearer, his eyes holding hers, and she could do nothing to break that invisible thread that held her glance fast to his warm grey eyes. Her mouth parted, and she passed her tongue over nervously dry lips, her eyes widening, heart hammering, as he came to stand in front of the settee, his hands coming down as if to embrace her. It was as though a magic spell held them both.

Then a car horn honked outside and awareness seemed to flood into his eyes, and the spell was broken. She heard his light laugh, heard him say wryly, 'No, I'd better not touch you—I still don't believe in you and you might disappear.'

'I . . . w-wasn't expecting you,' Tiffany said, her voice unrecognisable in her own ears, sounding cracked with forced brightness, her eyes dropping away from his.

'I trust you weren't expecting anyone else,' he said, which had her looking at him again ready with unneeded defence, but he was smiling, and she realised he was teasing her.

Then fortunately he was putting some normality into the atmosphere, moving out of the room, saying something about changing and having a relaxing evening. When he had gone, Tiffany thanked heaven for the chance to be on her own; she needed some time to get herself under control. Then knowing she couldn't sit around as she was all night because although her garments were respectable there was no mistaking the aim of their designer, she rose from the settee, intending to change into something less alluring.

She was almost at the door of her room when Ben emerged from his, his arm coming out to stay her. Just the touch of his hand on her lace-attired arm was enough to start her heart hammering away again, but she could see from his face that any effect she had had on him five minutes ago had now vanished, for his face was as composed as ever.

'If you're thinking of changing—don't.' How well he could read her!

'I can't sit around like this all evening,' she protested, though not as strongly as she knew she should.

'Why not? You look—er—rather fetching.' A wicked grin appeared for a moment, then he went on seriously, 'Stay as you are, Tiffany. To be honest with you I thought I might do likewise. Not the frills and fancies,' he was back to teasing her again. 'I was looking forward to a relaxing evening. You know, the slippers and pipe bit—not forgetting the roaring log fire.'

Tiffany fell in with his mood. The atmosphere was being made deliberately light by him; no need for her to run panic-stricken, he was tired and all he had in mind was to relax. 'You don't smoke a pipe,' she challenged, 'and anyway, we haven't got a log fire.'

They were both laughing when Ben said, 'You have no romance in your soul, young Tiffany.' But when he went with her into the sitting room and sat down with her on the settee saying he wasn't going until he had her word she wouldn't move, Tiffany ignored an inner voice that said she would be sorry, and agreed to stay put.

She had a few anxious moments when after his shower he joined her in the sitting room, not in slacks and sweater as she had supposed, but darkly handsome dressed in pyjamas and a dressing gown.

'I'll make some coffee,' she said, jumping up as he sat down in an armchair to the side of the settee.

There were at least two hours to be got through before she could go to bed without Ben thinking she was being churlish. How on earth was she going to get through them? she wondered, as she plugged in the percolator. Every time she looked at him she wanted to throw herself into his arms.

She dropped a spoon as a sound nearby told her he was coming to join her in the kitchen, but found she had no cause for alarm, for when he joined her, he was matter-of-fact, getting the cups down for her and telling her about the flight he had just finished, adding that his car had started playing up on the way home so he had left it at a garage and had come the rest of the way by taxi. As the coffee began to perk, Tiffany found to her surprise that she was feeling quite relaxed with him, even to the extent of telling him her flight plans and being able to ask him when he was next on duty.

'All being well, Tuesday, but like yourself, I'm on stand-by. Let's hope no one else goes down with 'flu.'

Ben was determined to keep the air free from tension, it seemed, and if his aim had been for her to get used to him sitting around in his pyjamas then an hour later his aim had been achieved, for Tiffany was beginning to enjoy the intimacy that surrounded them, and if her heart gave an unexpected painful tug at the occasional glance he threw her way, then it was worth it because not one angry word had passed between them. They could have been a staid married couple, she thought fleetingly, when he offered her half of the newspaper he had brought in, and they each buried their heads in print. She recalled he had said he wanted to 'talk' to her, but she put all thoughts of serious conversation to the back of her mind. They could talk to-morrow—tonight Ben wanted to relax. Burying her head in the sand it might be, but she wasn't going to mention the subject of her leaving, not tonight.

As she became aware of a stillness coming from his chair, a sudden clamouring started up in her senses. Unconsciously she had been listening for the sound of Ben turning the pages of his part of the paper, but she had not heard any sound for ages. It went without saying that she had been holding her part of the paper up as a shield, because not more than half a dozen words of the printed matter had she read.

She felt a tension so sharp hit her that she could almost touch it, and waited, the silence crowding in on her, for some sort of movement from his chair. There was none. Perhaps he had nodded off to sleep, she thought, and tried not to fidget if that was the case. Hardly complimentary if he was asleep, but Ben did a difficult job and needed to be constantly alert while working. It was no good, she would have to take a peep at him—if he wasn't asleep he could still be reading, in which case his paper would be in front of his face and he wouldn't see her.

Slowly she lowered her paper, and wanted to pull it back again quickly as she saw Ben wasn't asleep; he wasn't reading either, but was looking across at her, his eyes warm as though he had been willing her to look at him. Unspeaking they looked at each other, and Tiffany thought he must hear the sound of her heart beating madly away inside her when he left his chair, his expression gentle, telling her not to panic as he came over to the settee and took the paper from her.

'Not reading that, were you?' he asked quietly.

'No.' Impossible to lie.

Wordlessly he lifted her feet off the floor until she was semi-reclining on the settee, then he sat beside her, taking her trembling hands in his. Then very slowly he lifted the hand that held her wedding band, and almost reverently brought it to his lips. Still holding her hands, he looked at her, seeming to be trying to read what was in her eyes. Tiffany was powerless to hide that she wanted him to kiss her, wanted to feel his arms about her. The grip on her hands tightened, though in no other way did he touch her, but he was seducing her with that gentle, understanding look in his eyes.

'Tiffany,' he said softly, 'I want to make love to you.'

'I know,' she said huskily, while knowing at the same time that he was giving her every chance to run. She didn't move save to grip his hands with an answering intensity.

Without haste Ben lowered his head to her face, and she closed her eyes as his mouth came down in a feather-light kiss on her brow, to withdraw as again his eyes, now a darker grey, sought to read the expression in her opening luminous brown ones. He looked at her steadily, everything in his look telling her not to be alarmed. She felt him let go one of her hands to place his hand gently on a nerve that fluttered wildly at her throat, followed by a thistledown touch of his lips across her eyelids, felt his kiss transferred to the corner of her mouth, and in an agony of waiting for his lips to claim hers realised he was holding himself in check not to rush her, then he was cupping both hands to her face and without the need of thought her arms went up to hold him.

It was as if the clasp of her hands on his shoulders told him of her willingness to whatever lay before them, and with a hungry cry of, 'Tiffany,' his mouth at last found hers, and she was drinking in a sweetness such as she had never before savoured.

As their passion mounted, Tiffany was glad for Ben's experience; she had never been kissed in complete possession, there still lurked the fear of the unknown. As his lovemaking became even more intimate she could do nothing about an instinctive move to pull away from him, and feared he might have mistaken it to mean she didn't want to go any further, but looking up into the grey depths in his eyes, she saw nothing there but complete understanding. 'Don't be scared, my love,' he whispered tenderly, and with relief at his understanding came the release from the remainder of her inhibitions. She gloried in the feel of his hard body pressed closely against hers, and when he whispered, 'Do you want to stay here or shall we go to my room?' she wanted more than anything to be in his bed again.

'Your room, Ben,' she said shyly.

'Darling girl,' he breathed, and picked her up bodily, holding her against his heart.

But before he had taken more than one step with her to the delights that awaited them, the ringing of the telephone shrilled through the air, and he halted momentarily, the sound strident and an unwanted intrusion into a moment that was beautiful. 'No,' he said, meaning to ignore it, and carried on through into his room to place her gently down on his bed.

Tiffany could still hear the telephone's incessant call; whoever was ringing seemed determined to hang on until someone picked it up.

'We'll have to answer it, Ben,' she whispered as he joined her on the bed. She had come down a few degrees from the high plateau his lovemaking had taken her to and the harsh interference of modern science was keeping her there, but it would only take a few seconds for the phone to be answered, then Ben would again take her up to the heights and beyond.

His arms dragged away from her as if to say for himself he would let the phone ring all night without answering it, but for her he would do anything.

'I'll be right back,' he said tenderly. 'Don't move.'

Tiffany smiled a loving smile when he had gone; she had no intention of going anywhere. But she found when Ben came back into the room, she had very little choice in the way of her intentions.

'Sheila Roberts is holding on to speak to you,' his voice

sounded as though he was making every effort to keep it even. 'I'm very much afraid you'll have to go.' He came to her on the bed as she sat up, his arms coming to hold her to him.

'Oh, Ben!' Disappointment racked her. She wouldn't go, didn't want to go; she belonged here in Ben's arms.

He stood up with her, his arms still around her. They both knew she would have to go, no one was called off stand-by just for the fun of it, but she didn't want just then to be reminded of Coronet's depleted staffing, or the hundreds of holidaymakers having to hang about the airport if the necessary staff couldn't be called in. Ben kissed her gently in a kiss of promise and as she backed slowly out of his arms, his hand inadvertently touched the tip of her breast, making her ache with longing to stay with him.

Almost in a daze she found herself in the sitting room with the phone against her ear, and heard Sheila Roberts giving her instructions. With only a small part of her mind on what Sheila was saying, she was vaguely aware that the other girl didn't sound too pleased at the length of time she had been kept waiting to speak to her, '... and you're to report immediately,' Sheila snapped.

Tiffany wasn't sure what made her ask Sheila the question she did, a combination of the fact that she didn't want to go anywhere other than with Ben, and the knowledge that, like her, he was on stand-by, she thought afterwards.

'Ben as well?' she asked, her mind and heart still with the man in the other room. 'Am I to be on Ben's flight?'

Sheila's reply shook her to her very foundations, shattered the feeling of warmth, of happiness and eager anticipation. 'Don't be idiotic,' Sheila said nastily. 'You must know Captain Maxwell expressly stated that under no circumstances would he fly with you again. You know ...' But whatever it was she was supposed to know went unheard, for the phone was back on its rest and Tiffany was staring at it dumbstruck. All that was clear to her was that to have issued such an instruction, Ben couldn't think very much of her at all.

She heard a movement behind her, flinched when Ben's arm came around her, and hurt beyond reason, angrily shook his arm away. The flush of his lovemaking was still pink on her skin as she turned on him furiously, still in acute sensitivity at what had so nearly happened.

'How could you?' she flung at him, completely beside herself. 'Oh, how could you?'

'Tiffany ...' Ben stared back at her, not understanding, not believing the change in her. 'What's wrong?'

'How could you?' she accused again. The last thing she was going to admit out loud was that she was upset that he could make love to her knowing it meant nothing to him, but he knew—oh yes, he knew.

'For God's sake ...' he began.

'Don't pretend with me any more, Ben,' she stopped him, and watched as a hardness came into his face, but didn't care.

'Cut out the hysterics, Tiffany, and just tell me what I'm supposed to have done,' he said icily.

How could he have changed so quickly from the warm, patient lover, to this cold uncompromising man? She just couldn't bear to stand looking at him any longer, and with a strangled dry sob, she turned and raced to her room. Feverishly she began throwing the things she would need for the flight into her case, the habit of the last three years doing the selecting for her, and she was dressed and ready to leave without once having given thought to any of her actions.

Ben was in the sitting room where she had left him when she returned, but the fact that he too was now dressed was evidence that he hadn't stayed there when she had rushed from him. Stiff-backed, her eyes bright with unshed tears, Tiffany meant to totally ignore him, but he came towards her, moving a hand up to touch her, only to let it fall to his side when she flinched away from him.

'Now that you've got over your first burst of temper,' he said, his voice deliberately calm, 'perhaps you'll be good enough to tell me what it is I've done to bring this on.' Oh, you'd just love that, Captain Maxwell, wouldn't you! Tiffany silently fumed, and woodenly refused to answer him. 'Tiffany.' The way he said her name warned her she was on dangerous ground, though why she couldn't see; he was the one in the wrong, not her.

As he had said, her first burst of temper was over, but she couldn't bear the ignominy of breaking down in front of him, and she prayed she could get outside the door of the apartment without that happening.

'I shall be late if I don't go now,' she said firmly.

'I've telephoned for a taxi,' he told her, and as she opened her mouth to protest, he added, 'You're not driving anywhere, the state you're in. It will be a couple of minutes before the taxi gets here, so you can use those few minutes in telling me what's wrong.' An idea he hadn't thought of suddenly seemed to hit him. 'You're not upset because of what was about to happen, are you?' he asked, then, his voice changing to the understanding she had heard in it before, 'Sweetheart, it's . . .'

'It's not that.' Her face was scarlet, but he would know anyway once he got round to thinking about it that his advances had been anything but repugnant to her, so it was pointless to lie.

'Then for God's sake tell me what's wrong!' he bellowed at her, thoroughly exasperated by her icy refusal to tell him what had turned her from the passionate woman who had been in his arms earlier, to the block of ice standing before him now. 'I knew damn well we should have had *our talk* as soon as I came home, but I thought you knew how ...' He broke off with an exploding oath he didn't apologise for as the door bell rang to announce the arrival of her taxi.

Never had Tiffany been so glad to hear the doorbell ring, but before she could move past Ben his hands had descended heavily on her shoulders. She thought he intended to hold her back by brute force, but when she looked at him in frozen silence, it seemed to infuriate him still more and he took his hands away from her as though only by doing so could he control the urge to do her some injury.

He picked up her case, his face stony. 'Circumstances force me to let you go,' he said harshly. 'But as I live and breathe we're going to have a reckoning when next we meet!'

He ignored the taxi driver's hand stretched out ready to take the case from him, forcing Tiffany to follow him to the waiting taxi. Tiffany watched while he paid the driver, heard his, 'Wait a moment,' and then found herself looking into the iciest expression she had ever encountered. He took hold of her arm in a grip that threatened to cut off her circulation, and there was no doubting he was angrier than she had ever seen him.

'I could kill you for what you've done tonight,' he grated. 'You just stay put when you get home—or by God, you'll be sorry!'

CHAPTER TEN

TIFFANY was mindless of the route the taxi driver chose, was unaware of anything around her as renewed fury hit her. What right had *he* to get mad? Just who did he think *he* was? It was he, Ben Maxwell, who had made her the laughing stock of Coronet Airlines, not the other way about, for if Sheila Roberts knew, then everybody knew that Captain Maxwell could not bear to have his wife on the same flight.

How could he have done such a thing? And to think she had so nearly surrendered to him. Would have surrendered to him had it not been for that timely phone call. And what was he thinking now? That she was easy? That he had only to lift his little finger and she would come running? And *he* had the nerve to say he could kill *her*? Oh, what wouldn't she like to do to him!

How was she going to face the others? Those on the flight deck, the stewardesses. What on earth were they thinking? One thing was for certain, they were all well aware that hers was no usual marriage.

Her pride up in arms, Tiffany couldn't get it out of her mind. How willingly she had gone to him, had trusted him completely. Had even been glad that he was experienced. Oh, how he must be laughing at her naïvety! She was too angry to remember how patient with her inexperience he had been, how tender; all she could think of was that she was the wronged party, and to add insult to injury, Ben Maxwell was trying to lay the blame at her door.

Sheila Roberts handed her her flight programme when

she reached the airport, and seemed to have recovered from her earlier ill humour. 'Sorry to get you out of bed,' she said, the near truth of her remark making Tiffany turn quickly away before the other girl should see the hot rush of colour that stormed her face.

They had flown to Tokyo, spent a couple of days there and were on their way to Hong Kong before Tiffany simmered down sufficiently to allow a few doubts to creep in. There was nothing to tell from anything any of her fellow workers said that they thought her relationship with Ben was anything other than normal.

By the time they landed in Hong Kong her doubts were growing, though she still couldn't find any good reason for Ben not wanting to fly with her. She was good at her job, she knew that without being big-headed.

On the third day of their five-day stopover in Sydney, the problem she had brought with her from London had come full circle, and she was once again convinced that her action since hearing Sheila Roberts' news had been the right ones. Only now when it was too late, she could think of scores of cutting remarks she could have said to Ben, that had not come to her mind at the time.

On the fourth day she was again doubting that she was one hundred per cent right in her musings, and by the time they had taken off for New Zealand she was so completely confused, she deliberately pushed her thoughts away and concentrated on the job in hand. Not wanting time to think, she anticipated passengers' needs, made friendly conversation with any passenger looking a little lost, lonely or frightened, made herself indispensable to the crew on the flight deck, and not until they landed in Auckland did she face the fact that she was run off her feet.

She was pleased to find she had a room to herself instead of doubling up with other stewardesses as often happened, and she kicked off her shoes to ease her throbbing feet and thought to snatch some hours' sleep before dinner. But as usual when by herself thoughts of Ben hammered to be let in. What would he be doing now? His off-duty time would have finished; which route would he be flying? How many more trips would he make before his contract ended? Two? Three? And she wouldn't be flying on any of them. The last words she had heard him speak were 'You just stay put when you get home, or by God you'll be sorry', but he would have cooled down by now. Could she just pack her cases and leave before he got back? That was what she ought to do, but it was one thing to know what course of action one should take, and quite another to set out on that course. Would he be so very angry on finding her room empty, though, her bits and pieces removed from her dressing table, all signs of her occupation gone? For the umpteenth time, Tiffany turned over on her bed. He would most likely be glad, came the painful thought just before her exhausted mind and body gave way to an uneasy sleep ...

She awoke more refreshed for her sleep, showered and dressed in a calf-length dress that did a lot for her morale. She didn't feel like being on her own and knew if she wandered into the hotel's lounge or bar she was certain to bump into at least one member of the Airline's crew.

The lounge was empty of any known face, but on reaching the bar she saw most of her colleagues on her flight assembled there. They were out of uniform and for once behaving themselves—there was usually some member of the crew with a ready wit and in no time they were falling about and generally letting their hair down.

Fiona McKinley, a stewardess Tiffany got on well with, made room for her while Clive Winters went to get her a drink. That was odd—Clive had not said one word to her, not even to ask what her preference of a drink was. It was unheard-of for Clive not to make some come-hither remark, and she turned to Fiona to remark on it, when a glance at Fiona's face stopped her. Tiffany glanced at the other Coronet people nearby and saw one of the flight engineers in conversation with one of the stewards. It was obvious from the stilted way they were talking that they were not at ease, and her flesh tightened and she knew without being told that something was very wrong.

'What's happened?' Her question was directed at anyone who would answer, but no one did. 'What's wrong?' she asked more loudly. She looked at Clive Winters, who had just pushed a glass of brandy in her hand.

'Drink that down, Tiffany,' he said, a wealth of compassion in his eyes, then when she sat not moving, 'We haven't got the full details yet—but word has come through that an aircraft has come down some miles from here.'

'Come down' meant 'crashed'. Tiffany waited for him to add more, but it seemed Clive, having got so far, was loth to tell her more. 'Which airline?' she asked, surprised to hear her voice so calm when she didn't need him to tell her more —she knew, *she just knew*.

But the split second pause before Clive confirmed it seemed to go on for ever. 'Coronet,' he said.

'Ben?'

'Ben was the Captain, Tiffany.'

She had heard of people's hair standing on end with fright or shock, and actually felt her scalp move as Clive's words sank in. 'Ben was the Captain', he had said. 'Ben *was* the Captain'.

'We don't know the details yet,' Clive was saying with a kindness she had never suspected him of possessing. 'For all we know they may have made a safe landing.'

Only when she heard those words of Clive's did Tiffany's numbed brain begin to function again. There were so many things she wanted to know. Were they absolutely certain Ben was the pilot? How had they got the news? But a frozen calm had taken possession of her, and ignoring the brandy Clive was trying to get her to drink, a brandy she didn't want, she managed to ask:

'How long before we know anything?'

'Woody Carpenter is making enquiries now.'

She should be doing something other than just sitting here watching the door for Woody to come in, she thought, but she couldn't move, felt rooted to her seat. She should have gone with Woody, but how could she? She had only just learned of the crash. Oh, my God, Ben—she felt her composure slipping and made herself hang on. Hang on, don't imagine the worst, Ben will be all right—heaven help us, all those passengers. Ben couldn't be dead, she wouldn't believe that, she wouldn't! Tiffany fought for calm, Ben wouldn't want her to give way, but it didn't seem right to be sitting here in the bar with an untouched brandy in front of her when anything could have happened to Ben out there, but her legs felt too paralysed to move. She stayed where she was; she could see from here if Woody came through the door.

The next hour dragged on interminably. Every now and then one of the crew would go and try to find out more, but there was no news coming through. The bar was beginning to fill now and Tiffany was glad of Clive Winters' shielding form protecting her from curious eyes.

Then the door to the bar opened, and stayed propped open by Woody Carpenter. Tiffany looked at him, then looked past him and through the half open door. She saw the back of a man in Coronet uniform making some enquiry at the desk. She knew that tall shape, knew that relaxed stance, but was afraid to believe it.

Slowly she got to her feet, didn't hear what Clive Winters said to her, was oblivious to Woody Carpenter holding the door open for her as she walked through, and was within six yards of the man at the desk when as though sensing her approach the man turned round.

He didn't look in the least bit different. Tall, upright, the man she had married. Not saying a word, he just looked at her across the expanse of carpet. Then the ice that had encased Tiffany for over an hour melted. 'Ben,' she said brokenly, and ran the rest of the way into his opening arms.

Over and over again she murmured his name, all enmity between them forgotten as he held her tight to his heart. 'Oh, Ben, I thought I was never going to see you again,' she sobbed against him. She was mindless of where she was as her pride deserted her, and she sobbed for all who cared, to see, 'Oh, Ben!'

'All right, love. It's all right,' Ben said huskily, and hearing his voice when she had been having doubts that she would ever hear him speak again brought fresh floods of tears to her eyes.

And then she became aware that he was fighting to keep her by his side, as suddenly the whole foyer seemed to be deluged with reporters and cameramen, everybody asking questions at the same time.

'When did you first know anything was wrong, Captain Maxwell?'

'What was your altitude?'

'What speed were you flying?'

The crush was getting greater by the second. Then Tiffany heard Ben's voice, firm and authoritative, 'Just a minute, gentlemen. Woody . . .' She didn't catch what Ben was saying to Woody, but suddenly she was parted from him and Woody was escorting her to her room.

'How does it feel to have a hero for a husband?' Woody asked, and not waiting for her answer seeing her still trying to pull herself together, went on to tell her Ben had made his emergency landing without loss of life or injury, apart from a few minor cuts and bruises. Tiffany heard what he was saying and breathed a heartfelt sigh of relief, but couldn't assimilate the rest of the technicalities he was telling her. For the moment it was enough to know that Ben and everyone else on board had come through a crash landing virtually unscathed.

Reaction set in once she was on her own. Woody had offered to stay with her, but she had told him she was all right, but each anxiety-ridden minute in waiting for news of Ben had drained her, and as soon as the door had closed she began to shake uncontrollably, and it was far worse than any of the attacks of nausea she had suffered through her childhood. She tried to recall what, if anything, she had said to Ben, but she could remember nothing save the sanctuary of his arms holding her tight. Her world had been secure then, all tension and built-up fear had vanished the instant she had gone into his arms—thank God he was safe!

If Ben had entered the room at that moment Tiffany knew nothing would have stopped her from flinging herself into his arms once more. But it was over half an hour later that he came to find her, and by then her shaking had ceased and she had had time to collect herself—to sort out in some measure what his reaction had been to her.

To be honest, she hadn't given him very much choice but to do anything other than take her in his arms, she recalled, her face growing hot, for she was fairly certain she had launched herself at him. Poor Ben—trying to extricate himself from this marriage, and what had she done but staked her claim to him in front of all those people downstairs? No wonder he had called Woody to take her away!

There was no time then for further thought, because the door to her room opened, and without knocking Ben came in.

This time Tiffany made no move to go anywhere near him and stayed where she was on the other side of the room, the bed between them. She saw the slight narrowing of his eyes as he took in the way she was so obviously on edge, and noted the change in her manner from that short while ago in the foyer. She saw a slightly perplexed look pass over his face as if he was having trouble trying to sort out what to make of her, then knowing his quick-thinking brain, Tiffany made an effort to stop him reaching the correct conclusion.

'Wh-what happened?' she stammered.

'Downstairs, d'you mean?'

Tiffany flushed, knowing he was referring to the manner in which she had greeted him. 'I meant the crash.'

He didn't move, didn't come near her. His eyes were telling her nothing, but she had a dreadful suspicion he was just playing along with her, the reckoning to come later, when he said, 'I'm inclined to think it was turbine failure,' and almost offhand he continued to tell her about the crash. She felt herself relax as he went on, talking to her in such a cool way, that by the time he came to the end she realised he wasn't going to refer to what had happened before the press buttonholed him. 'There'll have to be an enquiry, of course, but with so many fail-safe devices on the aircraft, I can only think that a turbine disc disintegrated and a piece of metal must have flown into the fuselage and damaged the flying controls.'

Tiffany paled at what might have happened. Dear

God ... She looked across to find Ben's intent gaze on her and racked her brains for something to say—the whole experience must have left him feeling worn out.

'How are you feeling?' she asked, the growing silence in the room crowding in on her.

'More to the point, how are *you* feeling?'

'I ... What do you mean?'

'Stop prevaricating, Tiffany,' Ben said sharply. 'We've finished with the business of the crash, and now I think we have some business of our own to attend to—don't you?'

She was wary of answering him, and was glad the width of the bed stood between them, for knowing Ben, if she said the wrong thing he would be across that bed before she could move.

'I don't think so,' she told him slowly, then hurriedly as she saw his eyes harden, 'I ... I admit I over-reacted downstairs, but—but I wasn't sure how—how you would want me to act in front of everyone, s-so I chose to do the—er —loving wife routine.' She looked away from him, rather pleased she had been quick enough to think that up. But she was completely unprepared for the one word he threw at her, and her head came up sharply.

'Liar,' he said.

'I ... I ...'

'Shut up, Tiffany,' he cut into her. 'If you can't speak the truth, then I'll speak it for you.' Then with great deliberation he fixed his eyes on her and went on. 'There was nothing phoney, false, or play-acted in the way we greeted each other. It was honest and unpretentious,' and here his voice grew stern as he told her, 'I will not allow you to belittle the emotion we both felt.' Tiffany's heart set up a rapid tattoo at that, but she refused to meet his eyes. 'You could no more help yourself from flinging yourself into my arms than ...' something in his voice had her looking at him, 'than I could stop myself from holding you to me,' he ended.

The tattoo within her increased to the speed of a pneumatic drill, and was almost as deafening. She felt poised on the edge of something wonderful, too wonderful to be true, and was afraid to speak, frightened that anything she might utter would ruin what else he had to say. One wrong word and she could spoil the rest of her life. Wordlessly she waited for him to continue—he couldn't leave it there, he couldn't!

Suddenly, as if relieved she wasn't arguing the point, Ben gave her that half smile she loved so well. 'Don't tell me the fight has gone out of you at long last?' he said, his voice stern no longer, teasing almost. 'Are you ready, then, Tiffany?' he asked. 'Are you ready now to admit something I began to suspect that last time we were in London together?'

Her face flamed as she recalled without having to think very deeply that then she had been eager to give herself to him.

Ben appeared to be suffering no such embarrassment himself, as he asked quietly and deadly seriously, 'Are you now ready, Tiffany, to admit that you love me?' Tiffany shook her head, incapable of speech. 'Come here to me,' Ben ordered. Tiffany didn't move.

'All right,' he said mildly, 'I'll meet you half way—but no more,' and he moved to come and stand at the foot of the bed.

Even while her brain was saying, 'No—it can't be true, you're going to make a fool of yourself', her treacherous legs were taking her to meet him. He didn't touch her as she stood before him, though she was close enough that if she so much as swayed she would be up against him. But she didn't sway, and their eyes locked as they tried to divine the truth from each other's eyes.

'I let emotion get in the way the last time I knew we should have got down to talking,' he said quietly, 'so supposing you start by telling me what made you flip when you got your call to take the stand-by flight?'

Tiffany made to move away, her heart sinking fast; she'd read too much in his statement that he had felt the same kind of emotion as she had when she'd clung to him downstairs. But his arms came up fast, gripping on to her upper arms, refusing to let her back out of the confrontation, and she knew she was going nowhere until he had stripped her soul bare.

'Sheila Roberts said that under no circumstances would you fly with me,' she told him with quiet pride.

'And what else did she tell you?'

Tiffany tried to think, but it was difficult with Ben holding her arms so tightly, his eyes boring into her. 'I don't think she said anything else.'

'Then I'll tell you myself,' he said steadily. 'I refused to fly with you, Tiffany, because you were too great a distraction.' Her eyes flew to his, her heart a pneumatic drill again. 'When I'm flying I need to keep my mind on my job,' he told her. 'That was underlined today if I wasn't aware of it before—I needed one hundred per cent concentration to get that plane down safely today. Had you been on board, that just wouldn't have been possible.'

'I don't quite—understand,' she said helplessly, and felt a strong arm come round her, felt her chin being lifted with one hand so he could see into her face.

'Tiffany Maxwell,' he said clearly and distinctly, 'I love you so very much that sometimes when you're around all the discipline of my training, my upbringing, go by the board and I don't even know what day of the week it is.

Now, will you kindly answer that, because if I don't soon kiss you I'm sure I shall burst a blood vessel.'

'Oh, Ben!' He loved her! It was so much what she wanted to hear, what she had wanted for so long, for some seconds all she could do was look at him, only her eyes telling him what he wanted to know, then a joy so wonderful, so shattering took hold of her, she collapsed against him,

'Oh, Ben,' she said again, 'I love you so!'

Barely had the words left her than she heard Ben's exultant, 'Thank God for that!' to be followed instantly by his mouth coming down on hers, hard, passionate, demanding. She had no recollection of moving to the bed, she could have walked, Ben could have carried her, but she was lying beside him on top of the covers, feeling his yearning body trying to get even closer as she pressed herself to him, giving him kiss for kiss, her lips parting in sweet invitation as they swam on the tide of their heightened senses.

When Ben eased himself an inch or two away from her, Tiffany looked at him with a question in her eyes. 'I don't think lying on this bed is a particularly good idea at the moment,' he said softly, and suiting his words to action he lifted her with him and carried her to the easy chair and sat with her on his knee. 'This isn't much better for my sanity,' he grinned, 'but it's a slight improvement.' Then he became serious. 'I love you very much, my dear one,' he said, 'but we must talk. I want to get all our misunderstandings cleared up before I make you completely mine.'

'I still can't believe you love me, Ben,' Tiffany said huskily, marvelling since he had shown her only a minute ago how much he wanted her, that he still had the strength and determination to hold back his need of her and by so doing make their coming together so completely free of doubts.

'You'd better believe it, my darling,' he told her tenderly, 'because you're not going to escape me now—after all the torment you've put me through.'

'Torment? You?' And wanting to know everything at once, 'When did you start to love me?'

'Let me see,' he said as if considering her question, but when Tiffany gave him a little nudge, he stopped teasing and told her, 'Actually it doesn't require thinking about. As you probably know, you used to get under my skin whenever we flew together, and looking back I think it must have been pure self-preservation that made me hard on you. I know I was as mad as hell when your aunt came and introduced herself as my future aunt-in-law—but I thought I'd find out first just what you'd been up to before I laid into you. Then you came racing up to us in the car park looking as though you couldn't believe your eyes.' He gave her a self-satisfied reminiscing smile. 'I don't know which expression I enjoyed more—your look of absolute horror when you saw me with Mrs Bradburn, or your look of terror when you thought I was going to kiss you.'

All barriers down, Tiffany gave him a playful dig in the ribs and was rewarded with a kiss that might have gone on and on had Ben not been stronger than her. He returned to what he had been saying, his eyes showing delight as he looked down at her slightly flushed and beautiful face. 'The temptation to play you along was too much for me, I'm glad to say,' he continued, 'and then before I knew what was happening, you started weaving a spell.'

Tiffany couldn't believe all this was happening to her, and she looked at him lovingly. 'When did it start?'

'The first inkling I had was when you told me about Nick Cowley. I couldn't understand why, when I'm as aware as the next man what life is all about, I should feel all uptight at the thought of his daring to suggest that you go away with him for a mucky weekend.' Ben hugged her to him as she wriggled uncomfortably at that. 'Oh, I know you were all set to go with him, but you'll forgive me, darling, I hope, if I say you are a bit dim when it comes to playing with the big boys—a fact for which, I might add, I'm very grateful.' He pressed a light kiss to the side of her throat. 'I knew you were special when I asked you to marry me, and by the time our wedding day arrived, I knew I was going to keep you with me for ever.' He smiled down at her ruefully. 'Even if you did have so little faith in me that you couldn't see further than Shelia Roberts' half-given information— I don't know that I shall forgive you for that.' He dropped his teasing tone, and Tiffany saw some of the warmth leave his face. 'After all,' he said, in that 'no nonsense' tone she was familiar with, 'I ignored her, and put her in her place incidentally, when she told me of your mad fling with Michael Croft in Singapore.'

'Michael Croft? But I . . .'

'Went out to dinner with him.'

'But I didn't know it was going to be just him and me,' and she went on to tell him everything that had happened from start to finish.

'I trust you, Tiffany,' he told her when she came to the end. 'You didn't have to explain.' He gave her that rueful look again, and said, 'Well, perhaps you did, but I've always had an inner conviction that you wouldn't play around while married to me. Though that letter from Cowley followed by your decision to end things between us rocked me sideways—I'm afraid whenever I thought of Cowley and you, my worst instincts came to the fore.' His hand stroked the side of her face. 'Will you forgive me, sweetheart, for what happened after I handed his letter over to you?'

'Of course.' She'd forgiven him before he had told her he loved her, there was no question of not forgiving him anything now. 'Nick was only writing to apologise for being so horrible at Patti's party,' she explained, and was silenced as Ben kissed her. They were silent for some time as one kiss wasn't enough.

Again it was Ben who drew back. Tiffany's face was glowing with the ardour of his lovemaking, and she smiled shyly at him. 'I've loved you for so long, Ben,' she confessed. 'I was terribly jealous of Holly Barrington to start with.'

'Holly?' Ben exclaimed, startled. 'Good God, why?'

'Oh, I know now there was nothing between you and Holly, but when I first met her she was making an awful fuss of you.'

'Darling, I've known Holly since she was a tot. One of these days when she gets tired of running, she's going to say "Yes" to Ian Repton—you remember Ian?' Tiffany did, Ian had been best man at their wedding, but she had never suspected that he and Holly ... 'You like Holly, don't you?'

'Oh yes—who couldn't ...?'

'That's good, because until Ian finally ties the knot, I've a pretty shrewd idea Holly will be dropping in to see you from time to time when we've settled in at Linwood.'

'I'd forgotten—you're returning to Linwood at the end of the summer, aren't you?'

'*We* are, darling—I never had any plans to return without you.'

Suddenly Tiffany was near to tears. It was all so wonderful, and she found herself confessing, 'I thought you wanted our marriage to end—I thought when you spoke of taking over the running of the estate that you were hinting that it wouldn't be much longer before you had our marriage annulled.'

She blushed scarlet when he told her, 'You can get all ideas of an annulment out of your head,' and was thrilled when he threw back his head and laughed at her expression.

'The times you've nearly had your come-uppance, young lady!' She didn't need to ask what he meant nor to which times he was referring.

'Yet when I had toothache, you took me into your bed and didn't ...' Her voice tailed away as she was unable to finish the sentence.

'Darling, I know you're not experienced in these things, but there is a difference between love and lust. You were so obviously worn out with pain that only an animal would have taken advantage of the situation. Though,' he reflected with the honesty she knew was part and parcel of him, 'I was in a cold sweat when I woke up—thank God you didn't wake up until after I got out of bed!'

'I was awake before you, Ben,' she confessed quietly.

He stared at her disbelievingly. 'And you let my hand stay where it was?'

The colour rioted through her face again. 'I ... I knew it was quite innocent, b-but I didn't know what to do about it. I knew you'd be horrified if you knew, and before I could make up my mind what to do, you awoke and it was obvious you were more agitated than I was.'

'My Tiffany,' Ben murmured. 'Not only do you have a most beautiful face and body, my lovely girl, you also have a beautiful mind.' And he kissed her reverently. It was a moment to cherish, and Tiffany felt the prick of tears at the back of her eyes, then Ben was lifting her out of the chair.

'I don't particularly want to go downstairs again, sweetheart—I shouldn't think the reporters are still in the hotel, but just in case, would you mind if we had dinner sent up?'

'Dinner up here sounds fine,' she agreed, her lovely eyes shining.

'Good.' Only then did Ben take his arms from around her. 'I'll get in touch with Woody on the phone—he's got my bag somewhere. Then a bath and then ...' Once again

Tiffany was in his arms, the place she wanted to be. 'Sorry, darling,' he said, not sounding very apologetic. 'I've waited so long to have you willingly in my arms—I can't seem to help myself.'

Tiffany's eyes were aglow as they answered the love in Ben's smouldering grey eyes. The phone call to Woody could wait.

What the press says about Harlequin romance fiction...

"...exciting escapism, easy reading, interesting characters and, always, a happy ending.... They are hard to put down."
— *Transcript-Telegram*, Holyoke (Mass.)

"...always...an upbeat, happy ending."
— *San Francisco Chronicle*

"...a work of art."
— *The Globe & Mail*, Toronto

"Nothing quite like it has happened since *Gone With the Wind...*"
— *Los Angeles Times*

"...among the top ten..."
— *International Herald-Tribune*, Paris